D0562954

A Death in Tuscany

A Death in Tuscany

Dick Rosano

Copyright (C) 2017 Dick Rosano

Layout design and Copyright (C) 2019 by Next Chapter

Published 2019 by Magnum Opus – A Next Chapter Imprint

Cover art by Evit Art

Edited by Elizabeth N. Love

This book is a work of fiction. Names, characters, places, and incidents are the product of the author's imagination or are used fictitiously. Any resemblance to actual events, locales, or persons, living or dead, is purely coincidental.

All rights reserved. No part of this book may be reproduced or transmitted in any form or by any means, electronic or mechanical, including photocopying, recording, or by any information storage and retrieval system, without the author's permission.

For more information, go to http://www.DickRosanoBooks.com/ or follow him on Twitter: @DickRosano

To Nonno Domenico, in whose footsteps I learned to make wine

Contents

Prologue

It took a long time for him to reach this decision. Standing now, as he was, hands resting on the stone wall around this *loggia*, "his porch," peering out at the vines his grandfather had tended for so many years. "How will they fare?" he asked the wind that tickled his nose and rustled the leaves of grapevines heavy with fruit. "How will the vines prosper without Nonno Filippo to talk to them?"

The breeze brought the scent of evening flowers, sagebrush, and roasted meat to his nose. Could it be from as far away as Siena, lit now by the flickering lights of sunset, or from as close as the grill at the outdoor patio where his grape pickers gathered at this time of year? Or could the scent be stirred by his memories, a beckoning to his youth, a reminder of what life was like before he left this storied land?

The decision. It would become the most important moment of his life, but it took a lifetime of moments to reach it. After a childhood in the wine country of Italy, he had grown up in America, adopted its culture and accepted its passions, but he never forgot the passions of the Old World. He never forgot the lessons he learned from his grandfather, his *nonno*, as the Italians say, whose mastery of wine was itself a mastery of life.

The decision. It didn't involve only him, Phil Trantino, the heir to the family's wine estate. It involved everyone related by blood or sweat to the land that bore this fruit.

The decision. He knew from the beginning what it would be. Shaking his head at this moment, staring out at the vines, he accepted his fate. Then he smiled, because this was what he was born for.

The Way It Was

"Another?"

The single word was all I heard, but I awoke from my daydream at the sound. A waiter was standing next to the table, expressionless, but ready to take my order for another drink. The first Campari and soda had gone down well, and my thoughts at the moment seemed to beg for another glass of the soothing elixir.

"Yes," was all I said. I wasn't in the mood for conversation, but neither was the waiter. He walked away and let me return to my reminiscences.

I turned my attention to the blackness beyond the window of the airport snack bar. It was all a bit surreal now, recalling the years I'd spent working the vines and making the wines at Castello dei Trantini with my grandfather. He was dead now, the victim of a foolish accident at our family winery in Tuscany, and I was waiting for a plane that would take me home to Italy, to his funeral, to the empty rooms that once were filled with his laughter.

Although I had not lived at the Castello dei Trantini since I was a boy, my memories of it were clear. I could easily conjure up the morning mist over the vines, the blustery breezes that danced across the rolling hills of the estate, even the smell of the rosemary and sagebrush that lined the roads leading up to the Castello. But if, as some people say, the aromas of youth are with us always, I will always be able to imagine the scents of the vineyard and winery that occupied my early years.

It had always been so peaceful at our winery, the sort of peace that reminds you of how pure life can be in this world. My parents were living in one wing of the Castello when I was born, and even after taking up housekeeping in our own home nearby, my days were still filled with activities at Nonno Filippo's side. At the Castello life was adorned with long, lingering meals, weekly tastings, vineyard talk, and animated discourses about food and wine, all taking place under the medieval tapestries with scenes of grape trodding and winemaking that hung from the stone walls embracing the roaring fireplace.

In the flicker of candlelight, Nonno Filippo would wax poetic about this or that vintage. My father would argue about his choice of wines, others would take sides, or just be satisfied with devouring the wondrous meals that were served every night. Arms would wave, toasts would be made to settle a point, and by the end of the repast, everyone would be sure he had won the argument. Each would go off to bed, simply happy at the closeness of the family, the comfort to be had from eating and drinking well, and the inscrutable pleasures of life in Tuscany.

For us, wine was life. It was the substance of our being, and I expected to grow into the business and take over operation of Castello dei Trantini when I was of age.

Blinking away the memories, I came back to the present and saw that a figure had appeared in the window's reflection. When I turned, I saw that the waiter had approached. He could have just left the drink, but this time he seemed like he wanted to say something. Perhaps he noticed my melancholy mood. But I still didn't want to have a chat with a perfect stranger, so I just took the drink and turned back toward the window.

Sipping lightly at the rim of the glass, I let the sweet bitterness of the Campari coat my throat. It was the signature drink of Italy, and at that moment, I understood better than ever why Italian working men often quaffed just such an aperitif to fortify their spirits when sad, mad, or confused.

Settling back into my reverie, my thoughts focused on the days in the vineyard. I lived at the Castello dei Trantini until I was twelve and I remember well the return trips I made with my parents after our emigration to America, how I always looked forward to running between the long rows of grapevines and playing hide and seek in the winery. Even the aromas that waft up from the neck of a newly opened bottle of wine remind me of the childhood pleasures of growing up in so idyllic an environment. I'm older now, but the serenity of those times makes it hard to picture my grandfather being pushed out a window that overlooked the estate.

But, wait, I said it was an accident, didn't I? Perhaps I should start at the beginning.

The vineyards and winery at the Castello dei Trantini have been in my family for generations. My nonno, Filippo Trantino, inherited them from his nonno forty-five years ago, and he continued to produce fine wines in the quiet tradition of his ancestors. The estate represented an entire world to him and his extended family, but I had always felt a strong, personal connection to the vines and wines, and this bonded me even more closely to Nonno Filippo.

In fact, I had always considered him my best friend. When I was young, I would follow him about the winery all day, mimicking his actions — and cut a distinguished figure for doing so. When chastising an employee for a particular mistake in the winemaking process, he had a habit of standing with his hands clasped behind his back. S,o I assumed the same posture, standing at his side during the scolding, and would always elicit grins or outright chuckles from the worker being admonished. This would inevitably draw Nonno Filippo's attention, and his own amusement at the mimicry would terminate the session or have it degenerate into one of laughter and much joking about who was really the boss.

I learned grape growing and winemaking from Nonno Filippo during those walks around the vineyards and winery, and I learned the history of the Trantino family as well. He told me how his grandfather, Vito Trantino had started Castello dei Trantini many years ago, and how it had passed on to grandsons rather than sons. In Italy, the first son is named after the father's father, so every man's namesake is his firstborn grandson. Vito Trantino liked the significance of this naming sequence and decided that the winery would pass on through grandsons. As it turned out, his namesake was killed in an automobile accident, and Filippo, my grandfather, inherited the estate.

As a child, I would awake early each day and rush out to the fields to join in the chores of the day. The Tuscan sun shone brightly almost all the time and the summer weather was warm and soothing. Working in a field of vines is like other farming, laborious and sweaty, but being outside among those who were committed to their work made it easy for a young boy to be happy. And knowing that something as divine as wine would result always seemed to soothe the aching muscles.

Working in the vineyard offered its own excitement for a youngster, with no prodding necessary from parents to earn one's keep. So, I became a fixture in the annual cycle of the vines, learning to prune in winter, dress the rows in spring, nurture the fruit through the growing season, then pick the clusters of swollen grapes in fall. Making the wine was my greatest thrill, circling between the massive tanks and winemaking equipment while breathing in the heady fumes in the cool damp of the winery. And I was not deprived of my chance to sample the finished product, since Italians believe that wine is life, and even children should be brought up to respect and enjoy it.

Perched on the crest of a hill, with its long lines of grapevines stretching out in orderly rows down the slopes, and flanked by grey-green olive trees, the Castello dei Trantini is a place of extreme beauty, one you would expect to see depicted in the bright colors of some brochure inviting rich tourists to travel to Italy. In daylight, the burnt orange color of the stone walls stands in equal contrast to the green carpet below and the velvety blue sky above.

As the sun set, drawing the light down like a curtain, the lights of nearby Siena would blink on in the distance. This was a cue for me, even as a young boy, to go down the mountain and watch the sun set between the ramparts on the western side of the castle. As the last flames of sunlight were extinguished over the horizon, and the cool evening air swept in, I could hear soft music wafting up from the workers' houses along the crest of the lower hill. This became a solid memory for me, the bedrock of my life in Tuscany, and recalling it always made me feel closer to the land and to the Castello dei Trantini.

My parents, Paolo and Lina Trantino, decided to emigrate to the United States many years ago. My father had grown up in the Castello, the second son of Nonno Filippo, and as a young man he met my mother at the university in Florence. After their marriage they remained in Tuscany, and initially they lived in a wing of the family's castle. But as their children were coming into the world, my mother insisted that they live a discrete distance from the Castello to ensure a life of their own, so we moved into our own apartment in nearby Castelnuovo Berardenga.

After nearly fifteen years of marriage, they decided it was time to explore the opportunities that America had to offer. Their departure was ensured when my father was able to land a lucrative job as an engineer in Maryland through contacts of the family. So, at an age when I was not still a child and not yet a man, I was forced to leave my homeland and become an American.

I remember well standing beside the taxi that would take us away from the Castello dei Trantini. My parents were bidding final farewells to our family who had gathered for the occasion. My younger brother was already ensconced in the car.

I waited until everyone else was aboard to make my goodbyes to Nonno Filippo. I was already as tall as my grandfather. I looked into his eyes just as tears began to gather on his lower eyelashes. It was a quiet though wrenching goodbye, neither of us knowing how well we'd fare thousands of miles apart, but Nonno Filippo wanted to keep the momentum of our departure. After a brief hug and one last rustle of my hair, he pushed me toward the car and toward my life in America.

I learned quickly to enjoy my new country, but at the time I was dead set against it. America stood for the thing that kept me from Italy, from the pastoral lands of Tuscany, from the wine heritage that I had already come to embrace. I knew then that in the succeeding years, my rampaging down the rows of vines would be reserved for those precious trips "home" my parents could afford.

On each return, I would resume my shadowing of Nonno Filippo, but increasingly with an interest in learning the trade rather than being a cute — though juvenile — obstruction to the process.

My father had continued making home wine after moving to the United States, but commercial production was out of the question in our new home. Still, he preferred the wine he could make to the wines he could buy. As he always said: "If you make good wine, you'll have lots of friends."

As I got older, I considered moving back to the Castello and working for my grandfather many times. He made it clear that he wanted me to, but by the time I was old enough to make such a decision, I had made high school and college friends in Maryland and I felt that I was too established — and too American — to leave. Thoughts of Tuscany and the Castello were burned into my brain, but the jolt of relocation seemed a bit too difficult. In any case, I was sure that if I left it in the "past" part of my brain, I would get over the loss of it.

Then one day I received a call from my cousin, Santo, with the news that our grandfather had died in a freak accident at the Castello. His body was found in the morning hours but appeared to have fallen from a window the night before. Santo was calm on the phone, but still showed signs of nervousness that I couldn't quite put into context, and I hung up feeling lost and alone.

The news came with such suddenness that I couldn't contain my grief. Nonno Filippo was seventy-four years old, but his work kept him as healthy as a man of fifty. Of course, good health doesn't protect a man from accidents, but the prospect of his death was so remote that his sudden disappearance was impossible to grasp.

Recalling the Fall

In a family gathering that night, we spoke of Nonno Filippo and his life at the Castello.

"He was the cornerstone of that estate," my father said grandly.

My mother had great love and respect for Nonno Filippo but had spent relatively few years in close contact with him. She didn't work in the vineyard as I had and, despite her sense of loss that evening, I still knew that my grandfather's passing would have the most lasting effect on me. My brother, Mike, or Michele to the family, was unhappy but not distraught.

"It'll never be the same," my father intoned. "The Castello dei Trantini was his and his alone."

"But it belongs to all of the family," my mother said while clearing the dinner plates and wine glasses. "Nonno Filippo was only the guardian of the estate," she added, even while still acknowledging that he was the proprietor of record.

"Yes, yes," my father replied, brushing away her comment with some impatience. "But without my father, the wine would never have progressed as it did all these years."

Throughout dinner, our conversation centered on the somber news of Nonno's death, no one raised the matter of inheritance. Of course, my father and mother knew that the estate was destined to fall to me, but no one brought it up.

We talked about attending the funeral. My father couldn't return home due a persistent medical condition, and my mother wanted to stay behind to care for him. Someone had to watch the bookstore we owned, so my brother volunteered to remain in Maryland. This would ensure that I, as the obvious family representative, would be able to travel to Tuscany to represent the American branch of the Trantino clan.

"What do we know about this accident," my father pressed.

I was the one Santo called but he relayed only the essential information to me, so I couldn't tell my father much other than that Nonno Filippo had apparently fallen out of the window of the second floor. That the police had investigated and determined that this occurred in the early evening and the evidence indicated a tragic accident, without any indications of foul play.

It was later, once I was in Italy, that I first heard the details of the accident. Santo and his sister Rita took me aside at the cemetery. Children of my father's older brother, Santo and Rita had not grown up in the Castello, but loved it dearly, nonetheless. Santo worked at the Castello, managing the accounting matters and Rita sometimes helped him out. They weren't there at the time of the accident but had gathered all of the information to share with me.

"Remember the tasting table in the room, Filippo?" Santo asked me.

Certainly I did. That room was Nonno Filippo's wine library, and he spent many evenings there tasting different blends of wines from bottles standing majestically on a large, ornately carved, mahogany table. That was his favorite part of the day, and he spent it in his favorite part of the house. The wine library's walls were dark, heavy wood panels with exquisite carvings lining the edges of each panel.

There were two large windows on one wall, with low sills and two grand panels of glass that could be swung outward to open the windows to the fresh air. These were the source of most of the light, but a chandelier in the middle of the ceiling provided other, softer light, which could be turned up when Nonno Filippo needed more for the tasting. A tray with a dozen clean glasses always sat next to another smaller tray with a simple corkscrew, linen napkins, and a magnifying glass. A spit bucket stood near the edge of the table.

The only chairs in the room were placed around its perimeter, since chairs were seldom used during a tasting. In fact, Nonno Filippo was the only one who used this room, except on the rare occasion that he would invite the estate's winemaker or one of the family members to join him.

As children there were many times we — the cousins — spied on Nonno Filippo as he sipped wines in that hallowed room. He always seemed to be in another world, and it was clear he was as content as any man could ever be. Just as the furnishings of the wine library reflected his reverence for the activities conducted there, so did Nonno Filippo's appearance. He always dressed for these tastings as if he were attending a formal event. It was a ritual that he celebrated each afternoon, and it required ceremony.

"Well, close your eyes and picture him in that room," Rita suggested.

"What would he be doing?" was Santo's next question.

"He would be standing at the table, comparing the wines, and occasionally sipping from one of the glasses."

"What else?" Santo pried.

"Well," I continued, "then he would walk around the table to look again at the bottles on the other side. That table was too big to use from just one side, you know."

"Yes, we know, Filippo," Rita said, revealing some impatience in her voice. "What else?"

"When he found a wine that he particularly enjoyed, and one that he would enjoy drinking instead of spitting out like those on which he was taking notes, he would pour some into a glass and walk toward the window that overlooked the di Rosa vineyards." With my eyes closed the image was so real that I could see the smallest detail of my grandfather's appearance and behavior.

"Then he would stand there with his left hand behind his back, and the stem of the glass squeezed between the thumb and first two fingers of the right hand. He would look out the window, and occasionally take a sip from the glass, never taking his eyes off his cherished vines that stretched out into the distance."

"Exactly," Santo concluded, though I couldn't yet understand what he was driving at.

"What would he do then, Filippo?" Rita asked.

"Well, he would sip the wine until he had drained the contents of the glass, then he would turn and walk back to the table. He would place the glass there among the bottles..." and then with a nostalgic smile I added, "I remember how he would always empty all of the glasses into a silver bucket so no one could guess which wine he had deemed good enough to actually drink. As if anyone ever snooped around to find out."

"I did once," Santo remarked, recalling a grandfather seen through a child's eyes. And then suddenly serious, "What if I told you that Nonno Filippo's glass was found on the windowsill, and that there were still a couple ounces of wine in it?"

I didn't know how to answer, but I felt that this was not important information. Obviously, if he had accidentally fallen out the window, it should not be surprising to find artifacts of his final moments there. I told Santo this.

"Yes, but did you ever see him set the glass on the windowsill?" Santo asked.

"No, I guess I didn't. He did have a habit of always holding onto the glass until the last drop of liquid was drained from it. But what is this supposed to mean?"

"And what about this idea of his falling," Rita chimed in.

"I really don't enjoy conjuring up images of my grandfather's fatal fall, but if you insist..."

"We do," said Santo.

"Alright, I suppose he leaned out the window — and I remind you that he did that occasionally to inspect the work being done below — and perhaps leaned too far. Lost his balance and fell out of the window."

"The police found the fabric of his trousers to be snagged, as if it had caught on the edge of the stones lining the window," Santo said, and added coolly, "in the back of his trousers."

"And if he had merely fallen accidentally, how would he have had time to set the glass neatly on the sill?" Rita reminded me.

It was peculiar. The bit about the trousers convinced me that he had fallen backwards out the window, but he never turned away from the view until he had finished the wine. And the wine glass — still with some wine in it — was on the windowsill as if he had set it down in mid-thought, and I knew of no thought that Nonno Filippo considered more important than another sip of wine.

"Well, then what are you saying?" I asked.

"That he was pushed out the window," Rita said triumphantly.

"Why would anyone want to push him out the window?" I asked incredulously. "You can't even make a good argument that he had any enemies. All the employees loved him, the other winemakers of Tuscany respected him, his merchants always said he asked too little for his wines. He was roundly liked by everyone he came into contact with. Who would push such a man out the window?"

"We don't know," Santo responded, looking down at the ground, "but we were hoping that you would help us find out."

"Santo, I loved the man more than anyone," I said, almost pleading for logic, "but you are making some very wild assumptions about the nature of a man's death, declaring the coroner's report to be in error, and launching into an investigation of a crime that probably never occurred."

"It did occur," Rita said with an eerie confidence. "We are certain that Nonno Filippo was murdered. We don't know why yet, but we will find out." Then more timidly, "And we want you to help us. For our sake, but also for your own, because when the murder is proven, you will never forgive yourself for not having helped to identify the man who did it."

"Or woman," I added, my Americanism showing through.

"No," Santo replied quietly, "we know it was a man."

"What?" I said, startled that there was evidence not yet related.

Settling in Again

We continued this discussion on our ride back to the Castello. But, once there, our conversation was cut short by the stream of visitors who wanted to pay their respects to the fallen giant. The great room of the Castello, where the Trantino family had hosted so many celebrations with wine, food, and great cheer, seemed hollow that day, even with crowds of well-wishers murmuring their condolences to members of the family.

I greeted each of them with a perfunctory smile as they entered through the massive stone archway leading to the main part of the Castello, passing each visitor along to my cousins and other relatives, but I recognized few of the sad and sullen faces that came before me. I knew they were friends and acquaintances, as well as an ample showing of business relations who had bought and sold wines from the Castello dei Trantini over the years. The rest of the Trantino family seemed to know them well and I soon tired of the parade and wanted to sneak off to a quieter place to think.

Near the end of that very long day, I decided to gather up my belongings in the guest suite at the far end of the residential part of the castle and move to the foreman's house nearby. It was a sturdy stone building overlooking the vineyards once occupied by the man responsible for the care and upkeep of the vineyards. He lived there with his family, in a house given freely by the lord of the Trantino clan, and it was his as long as he worked at the winery. But, in time, the vineyard manager decided to move into another home near the town of Pianella. The stone villa stood empty for a while, but I had claimed it as my own during previous visits to the Castello dei Trantini, and I planned to do so again this time.

I got a ride to the villa from one of the vineyard workers. The little stone home stood on a level clearing at the top of a hill overlooking the olive trees and grapevines. On the horizon to the south, Siena sprawled across the hills in the distance, while the forests of our estate crowded in from all other directions. The prized *cinghiale* roamed through those trees and the hunt for them each autumn was a time of great camaraderie and challenge, rewarded with succulent aromas of roasting meat over an outdoor fire.

I stepped out of the car and paused only briefly to take in the scene around me, then carried my luggage up the stone steps to the covered portico at the top. This *loggia* offered a spectacular view and, before entering the villa itself, I had to stop again and savor the vista. Memories flooded past me from all the years spent in the embrace of this property, and I gazed out at the pastoral wonder of it all. I was supremely happy with my feet planted on Trantino land, so happy that even the tragedy that brought me here this time was not enough to squelch my pleasure.

I slipped in through the wooden door happy to be there, but I wanted to get unpacked and settled quickly so I could return to the loggia — this time with glass and bottle in hand — and pass the cool evening hours with some liquid refreshment. So, I went straight to the back of the villa where I would find the bedroom I always occupied on these visits. The villa had three bedrooms, if you didn't count the small one in the upstairs loft, two bathrooms, and a small but functional kitchen. The main room included a couch, several easy chairs, a desk and a fireplace. Off to one side of the room was a table and chairs that served as the dining area. All in all, it was far too much room for me to fill, but I was the villa's most frequent guest and so I considered it my own.

I hung as many of the shirts and jackets as I could in the cramped armoire in the bedroom, then wandered through the main room in search of the pile of books I usually left behind whenever I returned to the States. Picking up one volume that I had started but not finished, I trod into the kitchen to see if there was anything there I could eat. There would always be wine in the cabinet beside the desk, so I didn't need to search too hard for a bottle of Castello dei Trantini Chianti Classico.

I opened the door to the refrigerator and was stunned to see it filled nearly to capacity. There was cheese, milk, fruit, a large bowl of olives, and several hunks of salame. I also found fresh loaves of bread and cans of coffee and other snacks in the cabinet above. When I looked over at the cutting board, I saw a note neatly penned in rural Italian script:

"Signor Filippo: Welcome home. I knew you would end up here instead of at the Castello, so I did a little shopping for you. There should be plenty food for a couple of days and by then I'll check in on you and see what else is needed." It was signed Elisabetta, one of my grandfather's favorite employees and someone who had always taken a maternal interest in my welfare.

I loaded a platter with a generous sampling of the goods Elisabetta had stocked, then added a knife and napkin, and grabbed a simple glass tumbler from the cabinet. Except for formal tastings, I was accustomed to drinking my wine out of plain glasses, a throwback to the instincts for simple living I had preserved from my grandfather's teaching, and delivered those things to the table on the loggia before returning to the main room for a bottle of wine.

I inspected the cabinet carefully, noting ruefully that there were only about a dozen bottles there and making a mental note to get more wine the next day. It wasn't the quantity that interested me so much it was the selection. I often drank Trantini wines, but Tuscany had so much to offer and I wanted to have more styles and types of wine at my disposal during my sojourn. As I considered this and pulled one particular Chianti from the shelf, I wondered how long this visit would last.

I didn't plan to stay at the Castello for more than a week, but the news from Santo and Rita — or should I say their speculation — made me curious, and I was struggling to decide how much time I could spend in Italy to investigate it. Since I arrived in late summer and the vines were pregnant with grapes, staying on awhile would also allow me to enjoy the harvest, the most romantic time of the year in wine country. I would consider the idea over a bottle of wine, I thought with a satisfied grin, and strode out to the loggia with my newfound treasure.

Dinner with Cousins

"So, then, how do you know that it was a man?" I began. Santo and Rita had agreed to meet me for dinner the following evening at Carlino d'Oro, a local restaurant in San Regolo, a tiny hamlet at the base of the hill on which the Castello dei Trantini stood. We wanted to get away from the Castello for a night, yet we couldn't get away from the subject.

Santo went on to explain that muddy footprints, the size of a man's shoe, were found on the carpet leading to, and around, the table in Nonno Filippo's tasting library. The police dismissed this as evidence, insisting that the weather had been bad, and even the winery helper who arranged the bottles on the table could have tracked in the mud. The tracks to the window were easily explained as those of the same person, since Nonno Filippo always liked to have the window opened for him before he entered the room. But we knew that cleanliness in that room was one of our grandfather's absolute demands, since dirt and organic particles would carry an inevitable aroma and would taint the smell of the wines. Anyone allowed entry to the room would have known not to be wearing muddy shoes.

"Okay, so we know that someone was in the room with Nonno, or before he arrived, and was wearing dirty work boots. Other than ignoring the rules of the house about cleanliness, what does that prove?" I asked.

"First of all, it proves that it was a man," noted Rita. I decided to accept her notion, in spite of the fact that a more liberated person might wonder whether a woman could also wear work boots. I had to admit, silently, that in this country, in this region, Rita was probably right.

The wine was already on our table and the liter of nondescript house red was already down to a half-liter when the food began to arrive. The Carlino's walnut ravioli with sage butter is a local favorite, and I couldn't wait to bring my memory of the dish back to life on my palate. "Just as I remember," I thought in silence, as the earthy flavors of the walnut filling mingled with the luscious textures and flavors of butter scented with fresh sage. The dish was topped with a few fried leaves of the sage plant, crisp and salty, and I had to close my eyes at the sheer wonder of it all.

Italian food anywhere has always transported me back to my favorite meals in my homeland. "It was simply delicious," I told my American friends, and although most agreed that Italian food was the preferred cuisine in the New World, many of my friends misunderstood the double meaning of my summary.

Italian food was delicious, but its flavors owed their success to the simplicity of the dishes. Herbs, vegetables, and fruits had to be the freshest available, and meats were cleaned and cured by centuries-old methods that didn't allow for variation. Italian cooks weren't interested in fads or food that had to be deconstructed before the diner could partake. Italian cooks also weren't tempted to douse their creations in heavy sauces or accompany them with side orders of "baby this" and "baby that." Italian food was honest and forthright. Simply delicious.

As I emerged from my reverie, I saw that Santo and Rita were staring at me. They weren't privy to my silent musings and probably wouldn't have understood why I found it so amazing to encounter fabulous food. In Italy, they lived with it all the time and, although few Italians would agree to leave it behind, they all seemed to take the largess for granted.

There was also bread on the table — many types of bread that crowded the basket. There was olive-scented focaccia, onion and rosemary Tuscan loaves, peppery rolls that fit in nicely with the red wine and succulent aromas that attended every dish, and even some rolls that seemed almost American in appearance. The difference here was that everything came right out of Carlino d'Oro's oven, and the bread was still piping hot.

"It proves it was a man," I replied to Rita, "but nothing more than a sloppy man. What more do you have?"

"Let's look at this a different way," Santo interjected. "Let's ask the questions as if we believed there was some foul play." Santo had always liked intrigue, and I feared that he would insist on infusing the recent events with some mystery to satisfy his hunger. But I also had to smile a bit at his Italian-accented use of that very American phrase, "foul play," drawing out the vowels to emphasize the drama.

"The rules about cleanliness apply to the winery and the Castello," Santo began. "The wine needs an absolutely clean environment, and all the employees know this. The fact that there was some mud on the floor in Nonno's tasting library suggests that if it was a field worker who tracked in the mud that person must have been so distracted, that he wouldn't have stopped to think about removing his shoes at the entrance to the Castello itself. If he came into the tasting library before Nonno arrived, it would only have been to vandalize something, or poison the wine."

Santo's melodrama was a bit excessive, but I had to agree, at least in part. Nonno Filippo's schedule was very routine. He always tasted his wines at 4:00 each afternoon, so an employee barging in before the appointed hour would not be rushing in to confront my grandfather. He would know that Nonno Filippo would not be there; he would have to have another purpose.

"On the other hand," Santo continued, if the man entered brusquely while Nonno was there, it would have been to attack him, not to poison him."

Again, I had to agree.

"We know the man arrived after Nonno Filippo was already there," said Rita.

"How do you know that?"

The plates of food were starting to arrive from the kitchen and, with them, the waiter I'd come to know over the years of visiting the estate and frequenting Carlino d'Oro. Raffaello was in his sixties, at least, and one of the greatest assets to the restaurant. His smile was constant, and natural, and he greeted us like old friends.

"*Buona sera, signore. Come stai?*"

He used the familiar form for "how are you," but in an instant his smile was gone. A cloud darkened his face and robbed him of his smile, as he no doubt realized why I was in Tuscany at this time.

"*Mi dispiace,*" he said in sadness, adding in halting English, "Grandfather was a very special man. I'm so sorry for loss." He said this shaking his head, and even the awkwardness of his English didn't detract from his sincerity.

"*E tu*, Raffaello," I said, to change the mood, "*Come stai?*"

He shrugged his shoulders, as Italians do when they don't want to layer their good news over someone else's tragedy. "*Bene. Grazie,*" he responded, but it was only half-heartedly said. I knew I'd see Raffaello more during my visit, so I decided to engage him at another time. Now, it was back to the details of Nonno's death — and to the meal before us.

My roasted veal and grilled asparagus smelled richly of garlic, clove and rosemary, and Santo's grilled fish with garlic and lemon added to the gustatory delight of the evening. Rita ordered a platter of assorted grilled vegetables to accompany steamed calamari, and Raffaello brought another liter of red wine without asking whether we needed it. He knew the Trantino family well and also knew we would want to keep the wine flowing.

"Anita was cleaning up some things in the hallway when Nonno arrived that afternoon," said Rita. "She opened the door to the tasting library for Nonno and watched as he entered the room. She told us that no one was in the room at that time."

We continued discussing this as we made our way through the gargantuan portions that were the calling card of Carlino d'Oro. The restaurant sat nearly alone in this very small town. There was a tiny store next to it owned by the same family, selling dairy and deli items and most of the sundries necessary for a small household. Across a piazza only big enough for two cars to pass, there was a church. Of course. This was Italy, and wherever houses were clustered there must be a church. But other than that, there was nothing. It was as if this fine restaurant existed simply to serve the Trantino family and their employees. In America, this would be considered one of the best restaurants in even the biggest of cities, but in Italy, where extraordinary food is all so ordinary, Carlino d'Oro could exist in a tiny village the size of San Regolo and still have enough business to make its owners happy.

"So, what do we have?" I asked while taking another sip of wine. "A man, probably a field hand or at least a winery worker, entered the tasting library while Nonno Filippo was there. He came in so abruptly that he didn't think to remove his muddy boots. At some time soon after that, Nonno Filippo fell backwards through the window, snagging his pants on the stone ledge of the window, and landing on the steps below."

"*Certo*," said Santo in Italian.

"Was there a scream?" I queried.

"No," from Rita.

"Did anyone see him fall?"

"No."

"Who discovered the body?"

"Unfortunately, it was Anita," said Santo, making the sign of the cross to bless himself in memory of that terrible moment.

I sighed. I knew Anita well. She was Nonno Filippo's constant caretaker, especially since the death of our grandmother, and she would have been especially distraught to have discovered his body.

"No sound, no scream, no witness," I summed up. "So, I suppose that no one was found in the tasting library by the time someone thought to look there."

"That's right," said Rita.

As we emptied our plates, the waiter brought a platter of cheese and fruit. We each helped ourselves to several pieces and poured another glass of wine.

"I have to admit," I said with raised eyebrows, "it does make me wonder."

We ate our last course and drank the dregs of the second liter of wine in silence, but my mind was considering all the possibilities. In a few moments, I realized that I had fallen victim to Santo's intrigue. It was just when he asked me to consider foul play that everything seemed to turn rotten. But it was also in his scenario that all the facts seemed to fit, too.

Staying On

The next morning, I sipped espresso on the loggia while listening to the sounds of the workers reporting to the fields to clean and dress the lanes between the vines.

In winter, while the vines slept, there was always much activity. Pruning was one of the biggest chores and cutting, trimming, and removing the branches from the rows of vines consumed the short hours of daylight. For a while at the beginning of spring, just before the first buds broke, there was a lull in the work, while the vineyard stretched and yawned as if from a long nap, and the workers prepared themselves and their tools for the long days of cleaning and upkeep the vineyard required during the summer.

But I arrived in early September, when the grapes were plump and the color set. By this time, there was more work to do to prepare for the harvest and the farm hands knew that long days of work awaited them.

Even though they worked from dawn to the early evening hours, it didn't seem to change the generally happy mood that permeated the estate at that time of year. There was something energizing about working at a winery, especially as harvest approached.

I often told people that no one in the food and wine business seemed to be unhappy. That rule applied doubly for those working closer to the source, the farmers and vintners who tended the vines and turned grapes into wine.

Some of the workers recognized me and waved, but most were too wrapped up in conversation with their fellows to notice me peering out from the villa on the hill. A tractor rumbled noisily by, rocking rhythmically over the dirt road that led to the vineyard.

I was accustomed to rising early from my childhood, and being at the Castello again reminded me of the sheer joy of waking early enough to breathe the fresh morning air and watch the dew dry on the vines.

Sitting there, I decided that I couldn't go home to America yet. I was interested in Santo and Rita's theory in this case, and certainly wanted to put the matter to rest if I could. And, I had quickly resumed the pattern of daily life at the Castello.

As an adult, I probably appreciated the wine, food, and culture of the Tuscans more than as a child, and each time I visited, the pull was greater. On this particular trip, I couldn't help pondering my role in the estate and I enjoyed reflecting on my inherited position.

Nothing had been said of it yet, out of respect for Nonno Filippo, but I was next in line to inherit the Castello dei Trantini. Well, not all of it, of course, because my grandfather had maintained the estate as family property, and we all had a stake in it. But Nonno Filippo was the titular head of the Castello and the majority holder in the enterprise, and his position would pass on to the first son's first son — me.

Surely, Santo and Rita knew this and probably assumed that I would take over our grandfather's position in the estate. But I was an American now and my immediate family lived in Maryland. Being single, I didn't have a wife or children to consult on the decision, but moving back to Italy would still require a big adjustment.

Peering into the dregs of espresso left in the bottom of the cup, I smiled a bit at the thought. For years I had pined for my lost home in Tuscany, idealizing it in tales told to my friends in America, sometimes even arguing with my parents about why they ever decided to leave the Castello dei Trantini.

I called Santo later that morning and told him that I would be staying on for a while. He chuckled but then admitted that he had always expected me to stay.

"You're the *capo*, now," he said, "what you Americans call the boss. It's only a matter of some paperwork, but the responsibility for the Castello dei Trantini and majority stockholder passes to you."

I held the phone gingerly against my ear, hearing his words and letting the true meaning sink in for the first time. The Castello was now mine if I wanted it. For years, my dreams had centered on returning to the estate, and I would have been happy if Nonno Filippo had lived forever, but he didn't.

"Filippo?" I heard Santo's voice in my ear and regained my sense of the present.

"Yeah," I answered dully, as if I was waking from a deep sleep. But I quickly regained my senses. "I'm not thinking of that right now and maybe you shouldn't either. We've got to find out more about the accident. I'll visit the police this afternoon," and I nestled the receiver back on the cradle.

I stepped out into the warm sunshine and took in the view before me. It was like a medieval painting that's come alive — the rolling hills, brilliantly blue skies, and green stripes of vines cutting across the dust-colored soil. Twittering overhead were songbirds, providing the music for the field hands who worked in the vineyards. Old wooden carts were pulled behind diesel-driven tractors that puffed black balls of smoke with each rattle of the suspension bearing the load across the rutted road.

It was the pace of this life that was so attractive. When you grow things for a living, you become accustomed to taking time with your work. The plants don't grow in a day, and their progress is sometimes imperceptible, and Italians have modeled their lives after this agricultural instinct. Many Americans like to think that Italians are lazy or that they're not interested in the progress that can be had with frenetic activity. Italians scoff at the idea. Life is to be savored, they'd say. So, work should come at an even pace, and we should watch the plants grow and enjoy the pleasures they give us.

The telephone rang again, and certain it was Santo with a new fact to throw my way, I answered it, "Yes, Santo?"

A brief silence, then my father's voice came over the line. "Oh, sorry, Dad. I've been talking to Santo and thought he was calling back. How are you and mom doing?"

"We're fine. How is the estate, and how are you doing there?"

I explained to my father what I had heard, that there was a disagreement between the police and my cousins as to the cause of death, and that I had decided to stay in Tuscany a bit longer than planned to see what I could find out.

"How long?" he asked.

"I can't tell just yet, maybe a few weeks."

Another silence on the phone, and it didn't take long for me to guess my father's next question.

"Are you going to take your inheritance?"

A mixture of family pride and fear at my moving to Italy created a texture to his voice that was palpable, even across phone wires.

"Dad, it's not time to think about that yet but, yes, some decision will have to be made."

After completing the call with my father, I walked up the hill to the Castello.

With my decision to stay, I thought it was important that I spend time at the Castello, re-establish my relationship with Anita and the other household staff, and begin asking questions. I entered through the massive iron gate that kept out idle wanderers and tourists who thought this grand castle on the hill was just another Italian ruin. Once inside the portal, I heard the heavy gates close again by electric motor and clank shut. I strode up the gentle incline to the large carved wood doors at the entrance to the residence and let myself in.

The cool air inside this stone fortress was soothing, and the subtle smells given off by a building of this age were as familiar to me as any in America. I walked past the paintings on the walls and the antique furnishings in the parlor, reaching the back of the residence in only a minute or so. There, I swung open the doors leading out onto the veranda.

The Castello, more than any other place on the estate, gave me a sense of returning home rather than merely visiting. I looked about the room at all the things that had become a part of my Italian life, and memories of Nonno Filippo flooded back. I closed my eyes and pictured him standing at the edge of the rows of vines while I, as a child, dashed under and between the vines yelling for him to come and get me. I remembered the nights sitting next to him on the couch in the parlor of the Castello, watching the flames in the fireplace lick the wood stacked generously there, and listening to the stories my grandfather told of the winemakers of Tuscany. How they fought the insects, the merchants, and finally the government. How they always seemed destined to lose, but how they always won. When he talked about how the juice of the grape started in the soil, rose up through the vines, and was captured by the grapes, I could almost imagine it in my mind. He said that the grapes were merely nature's containers for the juice, and that the best winemakers only tapped this reservoir and let the juice turn itself into wine. *The best winemakers.*

I stood in the doorway of the parlor that looked out onto the vines. The vineyards directly in front of the Castello were dedicated to San-giovese, the regal grape of Chianti, taking its name from the "blood of Jove," and the grape, which had made the estate famous throughout the world.

I watched with interest as the vineyard workers moved about the vines with hoes and large wicker baskets for twigs and weeds strapped to their backs. They were checking the leaf cover on the vines one last time, making sure that the grapes got enough sunshine for the crucial time before harvest. With too many leaves the grapes would not mature; with too few they would shrivel in the afternoon sun.

Far off to the right and behind this vineyard I could see the Terra e Cielo vineyard, called that, Land and Sky, because the rows of vines climbed a small hill, arched over its summit, and continued down the opposite side, almost as if they were pulling at their roots to reach the clouds. It was here that the Trantino family grew its white grapes, and where there was already much activity between workers and tractors. The harvest of white grapes had already begun and, although it was a small crop for the estate, it yielded a simple, yet popular wine bottled under a separate label. Most of this wine was sold locally, some of it in bulk, and quite a bit would appear in label-less carafes on the tables of restaurants scattered around the nearby town of Castelnuovo Berardenga.

The workers passed among the vines with baskets on their backs, baskets which held the bunches of grapes they had picked. When the baskets were filled from their back-breaking labors, they would tread toward the trucks waiting at the outskirts of the vineyard, climb the wooden ladders leaning against the sides of the trucks and, with a massive shrug, empty the contents of the basket into the waiting hopper below.

I stood on the same side of the Castello as the wine library, one floor above, and therefore the scene outside was essentially identical to the one my grandfather last saw. He may have witnessed the first days of the white grape harvest, and undoubtedly nodded with satisfaction as he watched the work progressing in the Sangiovese vineyard. But he ran out of vintages with that fall from the heights. It reminded me of something said by Martin Ray, a famous though somewhat reclusive American winemaker. "In winegrowing you have but one chance a year," he said, "and in an entire lifetime, a winegrower has only a comparatively few vintages."

"*Buon giorno, signore*," came a soft but confident voice behind me. I knew before turning around that it was Anita.

"*Buon giorno, signora*," I responded, walking over to greet her. Shaking hands was customary in America, but there were still vestiges of class-conscious tradition in Italy, especially in a place like the Castello dei Trantini with such a long history. So, I didn't shake Anita's hand, but merely approached her to talk. She stood there with a broom and dusting rag and seemed intent on beginning her daily chores.

"I'm very sorry for your loss," she began, but I interrupted her.

"Yes, and I am sorry for yours. You have been a part of this estate long enough to be part of the family, and I know you were dedicated to Nonno Filippo's welfare."

"Yes," she said, casting her eyes toward the floor to hide the glistening tears gathering at the corners of her eyes. "I cannot understand why this happened to him." She said this, shaking her head slowly side to side, then repeated the same words again. Anita was keenly distraught, missing my grandfather and possibly worrying about her future at the Castello. I couldn't help with the first, but I could offer consolation on the second.

"As I said, you're as much as family here and I hope you will agree to stay on."

As Anita looked up again, she eyed me with a mixture of affection and concern. Her head cocked slightly to the side, she was probably pondering her new position in life. We had maintained a certain closeness over the years, through her relationship with Nonno Filippo, and she appreciated that, but I could tell she also worried about how it would work out with just us, without my grandfather as the connection.

I, too, was reflective at that moment. Instead of promising her a job, I had simply said I hoped that she would agree to stay on. There was a subtle difference, leaving me more room to terminate her in the future if it didn't work out, and a subtlety that the lord of such an estate would be able to make without effort. I must have picked up such close distinctions from Nonno through constant contact, but didn't even realize I was doing so at the time. All my life, all those months spent in the vineyard, the winery, and the Castello, he was grooming me to succeed him and it wasn't until this moment that I realized how carefully he had trained me.

Anita served primarily as the cook for the residential portion of Castello dei Trantini. She was a robust woman of about fifty who often took it upon herself to tidy up the house during the afternoons when there was no meal to prepare. My grandfather seldom had more than a quick cup of coffee for breakfast and preferred to eat his meals at 2:00 in the afternoon and about 9:30 at night. So, Anita had several hours in the morning and late afternoons to herself. She didn't often leave the Castello, except to do the shopping every other day. The rest of the time she spent preparing meals, managing household chores not assigned to her, and meddling in a loving way with Nonno Filippo's personal affairs. Just as she assumed the right to tidy up his house, Anita intended to tidy up Nonno Filippo's life. He would always make a show of objecting when others were present, but when he thought they were alone, he would accept her chiding with a satisfied — yet resigned — look on his face.

"I would like to speak to the police who investigated Nonno Filippo's death, Anita. Do you know their names?"

"*Sì*, Signor Filippo. The one in charge is named Franco Mirelli."

"Good. Thank you, Anita." Her apparent absence of feeling made me want to change the subject, and so I added, "You know, Anita, you do not have to clean the house. Nonno Filippo…"

"*Sì*," she responded warmly, "Nonno Filippo always said the same thing. But I cannot just sit around, can I? If there is work to do, why shouldn't it be done?"

Her look reassured me, and I realized that continuing with the usual chores of the Castello relieved the tension and loss that we both felt. Somehow, I envied her and wished that I could resume my usual schedule to dull the hurt I felt.

Down to the Winery

Before leaving for Castelnuovo Berardenga in search of Captain Mirelli, I decided to head down to the winery at the base of the mountain on which the Castello stood.

It was a long low building sandwiched between the macadam road on one side and a sharply sloping hill that dropped away from the other side toward the vineyards. This gave the property access on one side for trucks, tractors, and other vehicles used in delivering grapes and processing the fermentation, and a natural, gravity-fed option on the other side to allow the juice to be run from fermenters on the ground floor to finishing vats and storage vessels on lower levels. With less mechanical pumping, it was believed that finer wine would result.

I watched the trucks loaded with newly harvested white grapes arrive at the winery to my left. The little old man who appeared in the doorway of the winery was Vito Basiglio, the winemaker of Castello dei Trantini. I remembered with fondness the years I spent watching that lively old man skitter about the vats and presses, calling out orders to his apprentices, always moving and always directing the activities of the ten or twelve lesser employees of my grandfather's proud domain. Vito acted with such a feverish intensity that one tended to forget the patience that was necessary for the time-consuming production of fine wine. But he possessed the required patience also, as when I would ask for a taste of the wine when I was a little, wide-eyed apprentice myself.

"Why do you want to drink this grape juice when it still smells of the crusher?" Vito would say, referring to the sweet, musty taste of newly crushed grapes. "Be patient. We'll wait till it is wine," and his eyes sparkled at the mention of the word, "then we shall taste it."

Even now, as I watched him from the roadway, Vito darted here and there supervising the delivery of the new grapes, a man as old as my grandfather, but kept young by this annual ritual of rebirth. It was the process of creating wine that gave Vito his energy. He always looked so alive during the harvest, even though this time of year also brought the longest days and most strenuous work.

At one point, he looked in my direction and studied me carefully for a moment. Then, suddenly recognizing me, he waved with a broad smile across his face. Suddenly, his exuberant wave halted slightly, and the smile faded as he seemed to remember my cheerless reason for being here, and his arm fell to his side. With one last glance in my direction, he resumed his duties, disappearing inside the winery to usher the grapes along their path.

I went to the garage at the end of a short lane behind the main building and found Santo there talking to a young man in work clothes. After telling him I intended to speak with Franco Mirelli, Santo gave me the keys to Nonno Filippo's Fiat, and I went to find it. Parked next to the Fiat in the garage was a new Maserati Quattroporte, one of Italy's most elegant sedans.

As I admired its clean lines and stylish interior, Riccardo came out of a room in the back with a small bundle of short wires in his hand. Riccardo was hired a few years back to work in the winery with Vito, but his interest always drew him to the cars in my grandfather's garage. After offering to fix occasional automotive failures, Riccardo was made the regular mechanic for the establishment and took care of the farm and fermentation equipment in the winery as well as the cars of the estate.

"*Buon giorno*, Signor Filippo." Everyone at the winery had assumed Vito's label for me, the polite "signor" attached to my first name, and even Riccardo who was younger than I still called me Filippo.

"*Buon giorno*, Riccardo. Is the Fiat running well? I'm going to see Captain Mirelli."

"Oh, well, in that case," he said with respect, "you should take the Maserati. It's a fine machine, and you would command more attention if you drive such an automobile." Even though many Italians looked down on the *polizia*, posturing for people in authority was a part of the national charade.

"I hope that I won't have to pose to gain their attention, but if it is ready to run, I will take it. Thank you." The joy at driving such a car allayed my concerns about using something other than what Santo had suggested. He was so preoccupied with the affairs of the vineyard that I assumed he just hadn't thought of it.

I took the new set of keys from Riccardo and settled into the leather seat on the driver's side. Instinctively, I reached for the safety belt, as all Americans do, and noticed Riccardo eyeing me with curiosity. Italians drive like maniacs — well-trained maniacs it's true — but maniacs. In spite of this, and their penchant for speeding around blind curves and through crowded intersections, most Italians don't naturally buckle up the way we do in the States. Perhaps they think it robs them of some of the excitement of driving, but I decided to remain true to my American lifestyle and I fastened the seatbelt across my lap.

As I turned the key and felt the gentle roar of the engine starting, the odometer showed that the car had barely been driven.

"Riccardo, this car is brand new! Nonno Filippo has only put thirty-one miles on it."

Looking down at his feet, Riccardo responded, "No. Signor Trantino put no miles on it. Those miles were driven by me when I picked the car up at the factory and drove it here. Your grandfather looked forward to buying that car for two years, and when I delivered it to him, he stared proudly at it for a long time. It was evening, and at his age he couldn't see well in the fading light, so he decided to wait till the next morning to try out his new automobile. The next day he was quickly occupied with matters at the winery, then distracted by business at the Castello. It was that afternoon that he fell from the window."

Tears welled up in his eyes, and I could see how his love for my grandfather mingled with his love of cars, and I knew he felt that both Nonno Filippo and the Maserati had somehow missed out on something by not knowing each other.

"I was told that Anita found him. Is this true, Riccardo?"

"Yes. She came out of the door onto the veranda, the doors just beside the residence in the Castello. When she looked to the left, she saw him there crumpled up on the stone steps."

"Weren't the workers reporting to the fields yet? Didn't any of them see him?"

"There were workers in the field, but not many. And besides, the veranda is high above the vineyard, and unless they came up into the Castello and around the back to the veranda, they wouldn't have seen Signor Trantino. In any case, most of them reported directly to the winery that day to help with the white grape harvest."

"And what about Vito, the winemaker? He lives in the villa down the hill from the winery and supervises the pickers at the harvest. Wouldn't he have come to the Castello at some point?"

"Usually, but not that afternoon. After the harvest has begun and he is sure of the quality of the grapes coming in, he often leaves for Radda, making arrangements to sell the white wine from the Terra e Cielo vineyard."

Thinking once again of Anita, I frowned.

"That must have been hard on Anita, finding Nonno Filippo like that."

"Yes, it was very hard on her. She loved Signor Trantino very much." He blushed at the mention of love between those two, and retreated, "I only meant that they were very close. She was the only employee in the house, and they spent a lot of time together. They argued often, but it was the arguing between two people who have been together for many years...and loved each other." He shrugged mournfully at this description, as if trying to explain with his body language what he meant.

I didn't want to respond, to try to add anything to his description, but we looked at each other and understood.

Nonno Filippo was loved by everyone, his family and employees alike, and I couldn't begin to think who might have had reason to kill him. Then the words of my cousins came back to me, and I had to admit that the circumstances of my grandfather's death were suspicious. The police might not have thought so, but they didn't know him.

I returned my attention to the Maserati and listened to the sweet purr of a finely crafted engine. Riccardo couldn't miss the pleased smile that crept across my face and he responded in kind. He knew cars better than I did, at least as a mechanic knows them. But I knew cars as an Italian driver would know them. There was something seductive about such a fine machine, mixing refined elegance with come-hither sexiness and dominating power. A car such as the Maserati was meant to be wooed, not just driven, and could transform a simple Sunday errand into a memorable experience.

"Signor Filippo!" called Riccardo over the roar of the engine as I tested the accelerator. "Captain Mirelli's office is in Salina, just outside of Castelnuovo Berardenga. That is where the investigations unit of the polizia work. You can look for him at the Piazza di San Marco."

I put the Maserati in gear and, with a wave to Riccardo, sped out of the garage and down the road toward town. The car's low center of gravity made me feel like I was glued to the asphalt as it took the cutbacks and crazy curves through the hills and between the vineyards. The soft leather cushions and perfect spacing of gear shift, steering wheel, and accelerator pedal made it more comfortable than my favorite chair at home, and the exhilaration of driving such a finely crafted automobile had an unmistakable effect on my mood. Whereas I had felt a bit melancholy over the whole business of this trip, driving this car brought me back home to the Italy and the Tuscany I loved. There's very little more exciting than a fast car on a tough driving course through some of the world's most beautiful countryside. Of course, an Italian man would want to complete the picture with a beautiful woman beside him — and I did too — but that was a detail that I hoped I might one day fill in, too.

On the Road to Salina

The maddening curves and switchbacks are the best thing and the worst thing about roads in rural Italy, but driving them is never dull. The Maserati is very maneuverable, so I hugged the outside of my lane, trying to make room for the sudden appearance of a wild driver coming too hard from the other direction around a curve with little concern for safety. The ground rose up through the hills, then down again in a roller-coaster ride that is more thrill than fear, and suddenly I was winding my way down into the rolling green valley below.

Most of the land was covered with vineyards, an unending stretch of lines of vines bearing fruit that would soon be bottled as some of the world's most sought-after wines.

Perched atop hills to my left and my right were small clusters of stone buildings, of a color which made them blend into the rocky landscape but clearly of human design. Usually, these were small settlements that housed the crews of employees working the vineyards that sprawled down the slopes below. But I could pick out some older, and more robust, structures on some of the higher peaks that were walled cities dating back hundreds of years.

In medieval times, moneyed families with the small societies that made up their workforce were protected by these fortresses on tops of mountains. In the centuries that followed, these vast buildings and collectives turned into cities, with each successive generation adding new buildings that fell like stony veils down from the crown of the hill. These things were Tuscany's roots in the past, the castles and fortifications that evolved from military necessity to social convenience, a stamp from the antiquity of Tuscany.

The verdant green hills and mustard-gray buildings stood out against the blue sky as soft billowy clouds marched on toward the horizon. The Maserati seemed to pick up speed in the excitement of our surroundings and I soon noticed that I was racing down the road at a daring, though still comfortable speed. This car made driving easy, I thought, doing most of the work itself, expecting me only to point the direction.

As I crested a low hill and began my descent down the opposite side, I saw the town of Salina approaching. The golden dome of the church shimmering in the morning sun stood above the many scattered buildings, and children scampered across the roadway as they saw me approach. They had been playing soccer on a large open space that straddled the road, and they stood on the side, patiently waiting for me to drive through and vacate their playing field.

I drove past a few buildings at the edge of town, and then on to the Piazza di San Marco at the center of Salina. There was a large fountain in the shape of three maidens pouring water from jugs carried on their shoulders, and mothers watched while children played in the water the stone maidens provided. It was common in Italy to see such beautiful sculptures, especially in the village squares, even in small places like Salina. Over the centuries, Italian artists had sculpted thousands of these adornments and they were scattered throughout the country as if they had been sprinkled from heaven.

On the far side of the piazza, men sat at tables set close together, drinking coffee and gesturing grandly while they discussed a variety of topics from politics to sport. The appearance of a Maserati Quattroporte in their midst drew some interest, but after a few minutes they resumed their animated debates and I felt as though I had become just one more subject for them to discuss that day in the cafés.

The sun was shining brightly over the police station at the west side of the piazza as I parked the Maserati in front of it. Two men who were exiting the building as I got out of the car threw a sideways glance in my direction then returned to their conversation. The taller man with the jet-black hair and thin mustache was gesturing animatedly as he tried to make his point, while his lighter-complexioned companion walked along in near silence, smiling at times and occasionally getting a single word in among the stream from his partner, but otherwise serving only as the sounding board for his more loquacious companion.

I quickly bounded up the steps and went through the door. The lobby to the police station was dimly lit and there was a ceiling fan turning slowly to distribute the dank air in the room. After my eyes adjusted to the low light, I approached the lone desk at the far end of the room, just below the stairway leading to the single story above the ground floor.

A uniformed man with a very serious disposition listened to my request to see Signor Franco Mirelli, and he peered at me as if I was some curiosity. It wasn't the nature of the request itself; rather, it was the fact that I was asking him to do something, anything. In Italy, clerks have a sinister way of communicating to the people standing before them that they, the clerks, are not there to help us, and if they do anything in response to our questions, it is out of generosity or — perhaps — a momentary sense of boredom. This clerk treated me in just that way, cocking his head slightly to the side and regarding me with only a little interest while he decided whether my request was sufficiently compelling to make him rise from the chair and fetch Signor Mirelli.

Without commenting on my question, he slowly rose and exited the room. I could only hope that his movement was a positive sign of action on my behalf.

Soon a middle-age man with gray hair and a crisply trimmed, black mustache appeared at the door behind the desk, followed the finger pointed in my direction, and walked over to me.

"*Buon giorno*, Signor Trantino. I am Franco Mirelli," he said extending his hand. "I'm so sorry about your grandfather."

"Yes, it was very unfortunate. Can we speak in private?"

"Yes," he said, hesitantly. "Please follow me."

As we entered the room to the left of the dispatcher's desk, Mirelli closed the door then beckoned me to sit at the table and seated himself across from me.

"Now, Signor Trantino, how can I help you?"

"My cousins have told me that you consider my grandfather's death to have been an accident."

"Yes, this is true," he answered, sitting back, as if he knew what the next statement would be. "And you do not?"

"I have no opinion yet, but there are certain things that cannot be explained."

"Like what, Signor Trantino?" he asked, sitting forward again.

"Well, like the half-full glass of wine on the window sill, the pulls in my grandfather's trousers, and —"

"But we have already discussed these matters with your cousin, Santo, and his sister. The trousers were undoubtedly snagged on the stones of the windowsill as your grandfather fell out. As for the half-full glass... well, he couldn't be expected to drain the wine as he was making such an unusual exit, could he?" This he said with a careless grin then caught himself and resumed his serious tone.

"But we know that my grandfather never set the glass down," I retorted. "After tasting many wines and blends at the table, he always chose the one he liked best, filled a glass full of that wine, and drank it while he looked out the window at the vineyards. Something, or someone, caused him to put it down."

"Something, yes," Mirelli interjected. "Perhaps deciding that the wine was not so perfect after all."

"He always held it in his right hand. The glass was found on the left side of the windowsill."

"Signor Trantino, how do you know that he never put the glass down? I thought Santo said that your grandfather preferred to taste these wines in private."

"He did, but as children we were adventurous and a little curious about what Nonno Filippo did in that hallowed room. We hid in the closet that is to the left of the door and watched him as he tasted the wines and then selected one to drink. He always stood at the window with the glass in his right hand and his left hand behind his back as he observed the activities in the vineyard below. He never put the glass down until he finished the wine in it, and then he would return the glass to the table, sometimes hiding it mischievously among the other glasses, and leave the room. This pattern never varied."

"And how many times did you observe it?" Mirelli asked.

"A few. I don't know, maybe five or six. After a while, we realized that there was nothing mysterious going on in the room, so we lost interest. Children do that you know."

"Yes," he added, rubbing his chin, "children do lose interest. But sometimes I wish adults would. Signor Trantino, as a child you watched your grandfather drink wine a few times and from that you think that any variation in his behavior suggests some nefarious act. I wish police work was so simple, then I would be able to solve all these cases and spend more time with my family."

"But don't you even care? Shouldn't you investigate the possibility?"

"Yes, we should, and we did. We spent many hours after his death questioning people, and not once did we come up with a motive. Not even a suspect. Signor Trantino, everyone loved your grandfather. We couldn't find anyone who had a reason to murder him. Why should we assume he was killed by someone if we can't find anyone who wanted to kill him?"

I was silent for a moment, pondering his statements and deciding on the best time to discuss the footprints. But I held back.

Mirelli stood up and motioned to the door. As he followed me through the front room with the dispatcher and the other polizia milling about, I decided to play my trump card at the last possible moment. Soon, I was settling once again into the deep luxury of the Maserati, and Mirelli was pushing on the door to shut it, unable to disguise his admiration for the automobile.

"Signor Mirelli," I began, looking up at the gray-headed figure looming over me, "how did you explain the footprints?"

"The weather had been bad here for weeks. More rain than we need, and certainly more than the vineyards want. We were all tracking mud into our homes and offices."

"But Nonno Filippo would never have allowed his tasting room to be soiled with mud. Everything has an odor, he always said, and I'm sure dirt was on that list."

"That's fine for your grandfather, and I'm sure he wiped his feet when he entered. But what about everyone else?"

"Only one other person went in there. Beppo, the man who sets up the bottles and glasses for my grandfather. Did you question him?"

"Yes," Mirelli responded thoughtfully. "He was even insulted that I would ask him about the mud stains."

"Insulted?"

"Yes. He said he would never allow dirt of any kind to enter that room," he said with great concentration, rubbing his chin once more.

I started the motor of the Maserati and looked away from Mirelli and at the men still seated at the tables across the piazza. They watched us keenly, as if conversations with a police official following a suspicious death might be more interesting than yesterday's soccer score. I saw one of them point in our direction and nod to his companion.

"Perhaps we should wonder about that, Captain Mirelli."

"Perhaps."

A Time to Eat

Leaving Salina, I decided to spend some time in the Tuscan country-side. It remains one of the world's most beautiful landscapes, and lacking someone to share it with, I could at least enjoy it behind the wheel of this amazing vehicle.

Since I had left just after noon, I knew I had about two hours to tool the roadways before looking for a place to stop and eat. That was just long enough to get to Montalcino by way of a winding route that would take me in and out of little villages while I made my way through the valley.

Montalcino is another of Tuscany's many hilltop towns, but this one has the distinction of being the capital of one of the region's most famous wines. Brunello di Montalcino, the noble red wine made from the Sangiovese grosso grape, has led all Italian wines in pricing for decades, eclipsed only in recent years by the likes of Barolo and Barbaresco, and the town after which it is named is famous for access to this phenomenal wine. It's said that Montalcino is the only town in Italy that has more wine bars than churches, a notable accomplishment that becomes obvious to anyone who walks her streets and *piazze*.

As the Maserati approached the hills on which the town was built, I could see the eleventh-century *fortezza* on the crest of the hill. My eyes followed the line of stones that made up the outer wall of what was once a fortification against a Sienese invasion. Before entering the town, I found Boccondivino, a favorite restaurant of mine, and one of the best in the region for pasta with truffles. It was a bit too early in the season to have truffles, so I quickly disposed of the idea before my mouth began to water, but the thoughts of previous meals still made this an absolute stop for me.

Inside the restaurant, there were about a dozen tables, some just fill-ing up with people having their midday meal. There was the foursome of three men and one very beautiful woman. They seemed to be work-mates and it was obvious from the conversation that the men treasured having an attractive woman at the table, even if she had to be shared. There was the small family: father, mother, and two young children who were quieter but very involved in consuming what appeared to be the third course of a meal. There was the older man and young woman, pleasant and proper and yet intimate enough to suggest that this was a man entertaining his daughter. His comments were not romantic, but were about romance, and her facial expressions were condescending, accepting his comments without wanting to let her father think he was going to alter her lifestyle.

Across the room were two middle-aged women sitting together. Italy is not as progressive as America and, while the women here are strong and forceful in their own way, it's less common to see women dining out together without a man at the table. I thought for a moment that these two might be tourists, traveling together on a "no husbands" vacation, but let the matter drop when the hostess approached me with a smile.

"*Buon giorno, signore,*" she said. "May I seat you?"

"*Sì, solo per uno,*" I said, then followed her to a small table set against the window. I sat down, spread the napkin on my lap, and gazed out the window at the valley that separated this restaurant from Montalcino.

The sun was bright and warm now, and taking a break from the afternoon heat to partake of a delicious meal was a time-honored tra-dition in Italy that I intended to keep. In a few moments, a basket of bread and simple carafe of red wine appeared on the table. I expected the first, but was surprised by the second, until I caught a little hand waving out of the corner of my eye. It was the young woman I had watched being counseled by her father. She smiled at me and nodded, indicating that the bottle was from her. My eyes were adjusting to the light when I first saw her, and I didn't recognize her at the time. But now that I was able to see more clearly, I realized that this was Ilsa, the woman in charge of our winery's gift shop.

I took the opportunity to look long at her, appreciating the curve of her legs under the table, the way the soft light played across her olive-colored skin, and the long strawberry blond tresses that curled and bundled across her shoulders and down her back. I knew of her, that her mother was Swedish and her father Italian, which accounted for the magnificent merging of physical beauty in Ilsa, but I didn't know anything else about her parents. Apparently, her father was a bit protective of her, which I fully understood, as I drank in the beauty that she offered. Her mother, I was told, was also very beautiful, but spent most of her time at home. I didn't know where her father worked, but on this occasion at least he decided to spend the afternoon with his daughter and, judging from the tone of his conversation, to give her some advice.

I tasted the wine from the label-less carafe and smiled as I recognized it: the Trantini Rosso di Montalcino, from Sangiovese grapes grown not far from this very restaurant. I was glad that Ilsa would choose one of our wines to deliver in this anonymous carafe.

Ilsa soon excused herself from her father's company and came over to sit down with me.

"*Grazie, signore,*" she began, but I interrupted.

"Why are you thanking me? You sent over the bottle of wine."

She laughed gently. "Well, actually, I didn't send it over. I just happened to mention to the waitress that you were Filippo Trantino from the Castello dei Trantini and she brought the wine over herself. Could you imagine what my father would have done if I sent some wine to a man in a restaurant?" As she said this, her eyebrows first went up, then burrowed together in a cross look, at odds with the satisfied smile that crossed her lips.

"Then why are you thanking me, and what does your father think of you leaving him to go sit with a man at a restaurant?" At saying this, I shuddered, realizing that I might be sending her away.

"Yes, well, that is very funny, actually," Ilsa said. "I told my father that I was with you last night."

"What?" I said, incredulously. It was obvious that her father was lecturing Ilsa on the dangers men posed, and she had just made up a lie that made me the villain in his eyes.

"No, wait," she reassured me, patting my hand. "It's alright. I work at the Castello. He didn't know where I was last night, and I said I was with you. He thinks I was working, so he's not mad at me — or you."

At her last words, she let her hand rest on mine. Her skin was warm and soft, and I wondered why she didn't remove her hand but chose to let it stay there. It felt good and I realized that I was enjoying the physical contact more than she might have intended. Or maybe she did intend it.

"So, now, what am I supposed to do?" I asked.

"Nothing. I told Papa that I was just going to come over and say hello." Then she stood up and turned to leave. After two steps, she turned back, the fabric of her skirt giving a slight swishing sound as it played across her legs and settled back in place.

"However, if you want to thank me for my extra work last night, you could ask me to dinner tonight."

I was momentarily speechless. Of course, I would want to have dinner with such a beautiful woman, but her forwardness and easy suggestion left me without the right words to carry out the idea.

"Well?" she asked, giving me one more chance to succeed.

"Of course," I said, "You've put in too many hours. I think we should have dinner tonight in Siena." I now realized that she not only wanted a dinner date with me, but she wanted her father to hear the conversation. "How about if I pick you up at about eight?" I said with enough volume to carry to her father's ears.

"*Certo*," she said, and she spun around with a smile on her lips, long hair flipping over one shoulder and stiletto heels clicking across the stone floor to her table.

The waitress had stayed away for a few moments, aware that there was a rendezvous being planned, but now that Ilsa was gone, she returned. I ordered grilled vegetables, pasta with a vodka cream sauce, and baked white fish and avocado for the main course. My appetite had fled a bit as my stomach fluttered over Ilsa's approach, but it was slowly returning. I had often seen her working at the winery store, appreciated her beauty and considered whether to strike up a conversation. But I was always at the estate for only a short period of time and it didn't seem to make much sense to get involved with one of Nonno's employees, then fly back to America.

Then it dawned on me that I had just made a date with one of *my* employees. I made a mental note to be more careful in the future, as the capo it could be seen as improper — but I wasn't worried about it enough at this point to consider canceling my plans with Ilsa.

About halfway through my meal, Ilsa and her father stood to leave. They walked by my table and her father greeted me warmly, as an Italian man would for his daughter's boss and owner of a large winery. Ilsa smiled sweetly — and a bit seductively? — then left a slip of paper on the table next to my hand. After they left, I lifted the paper and unfolded it. It was her address and telephone number. It's a good thing that she was thinking ahead. I was so hypnotized by our encounter that it didn't even occur to me to ask her where she lived.

More Wine Bars than Churches

After a leisurely meal, I finished off the remains of the carafe of wine. Sipping a cup of espresso, I considered the rest of my day. I was too near Montalcino to pass up a quick visit. There were wine shops and *enoteche* that served the Trantini wines and it wouldn't hurt to pay a visit. Then there was the magnificent fort, the *fortezza*, I had spied from the roadway.

As I strode to the Maserati I mused over the difference between Italians and Americans when it came to dining, and particularly to drinking wine then driving. Italians were passionate about many things, but wine and automobiles ranked among the highest on the list. Consuming a meal without wine was considered somewhat sacrilegious, and denying a man an afternoon driving in a fine automobile would be cause for a fight. So, whereas Americans were always trying to put distance between alcohol and driving, the Italians never seemed to be able to.

I had enough wine to feel its effects and probably would have been over the legal limit in America, but it energized me and driving through the valley and climbing the hill into Montalcino seemed an exciting prospect, and the slight buzz from the Rosso di Montalcino I'd consumed added to the pleasure.

The sun was arching toward the horizon since it was now about four o'clock, and the heat had relented a bit. I rolled down the windows on the car and listened to the engine purr. Releasing the clutch slightly

I could feel the powerful gears engage and the Maserati pulled away from the parking space. The smooth transition from still to moving showed the strength of the machine, but it accomplished it without a roaring or whining sound. It was a display of subtle power, and with it the automobile proved itself.

The ride into Montalcino was short, with the *fortezza* and the two lone towers of the town always in sight. I pulled to a quick stop in the parking lot just inside the city's walls, paid for a parking stub that I then left on the deck of the dashboard, and walked away toward the *fortezza*. I wanted to climb the walls to the fort's battlements and take in the view of the valley while the shadows were not too long. Besides, I wanted to give the shops time to reopen before visiting them.

Inside the visitors' area in the main building of the *fortezza* is a wine bar. There they serve many of the region's best wines, with a not-so-subtle bias toward the Brunello di Montalcino and Rosso di Montalcino from neighboring vineyards. I scanned the bottles on the shelf behind the bar and picked out a few of the Castello dei Trantini labels, two different vintages of our Rosso and one Chianti.

The Trantino estate had never produced a Brunello, and so I knew I wouldn't find one of those there. Our vineyards were mostly in the hills surrounding the Castello northeast of Siena, which were legally in the Chianti zone and so we could only produce Chianti — or some other non-specific wine — from the grapes. Brunello di Montalcino and its lesser sibling Rosso di Montalcino were legally required to be made of Sangiovese grosso grapes grown in the district immediately around the town of Montalcino. When my grandfather decided to buy some vineyard land near Montalcino, he chose to make only Rosso, leaving the exalted Brunello to the estates that existed in the region. It was a nod of respect for his counterparts around Montalcino, and while it could have provided another revenue stream for the Castello dei Trantini, it ensured that our family would remain focused on Chianti and similar wines.

After purchasing a ticket to climb the stairs to the *fortezza*'s crown, I made my way up the old stone steps to the summit. There is a walkway that snakes all the way around it, with only three sets of steps hidden away in towers that would allow pedestrians to return to the ground level. I took my time, pausing every several yards as I made the circuit around the *fortezza*, taking in the view of the valley that spread before me. There were little villages and many farms, with a good share of vineyards planted among them. I could see the cars slipping around curves and across the broad expanse of the single highway in the region. Birds swooped overhead, and a slight breeze kept the flags on the battlements aloft.

On the other side of the *fortezza*, the town filled the view. There were narrow streets and tiny shops, intermingled with *enoteche* and *trattorie*, and more pedestrian and scooter traffic than cars. It was easy to imagine this town in its heyday when its population soared above thirty thousand, but now there were fewer than six thousand Montalcinese, as the town lost some businesses and kept only the vestiges of its former greatness. And this elegant decline may be what makes Montalcino so important. It maintains its claim as the city of wine excellence, the birthplace of the noble Brunello. As the town shed its other industries, its wine history came to the fore, and in recent years few people think about Montalcino as anything but the source of Italy's vinous excellence.

I descended the steps and stopped by the bar to sample a few of the Brunello. There was the Val di Suga and the Biondi-Santi, then the Castello Banfi, the estate owned by an American family but credited with making some of Italy's best wines. With this little mid-afternoon pick-me-up, I was ready to hit the streets.

I stopped by the Enoteca Francia and spoke to Giovanni. His shop sold more Brunello by the glass and by the bottle than any establishment in town — and probably any in Tuscany.

"*Sì*, signore," he said when I asked about the Trantini wines. "Of course, we carry them."

As Giovanni reached behind the counter to produce a bottle of the Rosso and one of our Chianti Classico, he cast a suspicious glance back at me.

"But you are Signor Trantino himself," he said, as if he was suddenly surprised that he recognized me. "Signor Filippo, *come stai*?" he asked.

"*Sì*, but I'm just visiting, and I wanted to check on our wines. How are they received here?"

"Oh, very well! The people who come in asking for Chianti often ask for the Trantini wines, if they know Chianti at all. However," he added, with a smile and a shrug of his shoulders, "people usually come here looking for Brunello." This last comment was made with eyebrows raised, as if what he was saying was so obvious he didn't think he needed to remind me.

"Yes, I know, and that's what I expect. How about the Rosso di Montalcino? You must sell a lot of that, at least to the customers who don't want to spend so much. *Non e' vero*?" I asked.

"Yes, it's true. Rosso sells very well," adding with a conspiratorial tone, "and we know it's a better deal anyway, no?"

"*Sì*, it's a better deal." I paused, then Giovanni got that I was asking about the Trantini Rosso. Our Chianti and Chianti Classico and other wines from the estate are bottled as Castello dei Trantini wines, but the label on the Rosso di Montalcino says simply Trantini, to further disassociate it from the estate and the Castello that watches over the vines near our home.

"*Sì*, the Trantini Rosso sells, but not as well as the Chianti. It's very good," Giovanni quickly added, so as not to insult me, "but your Chianti is magnifico and everyone thinks of it first when they hear the name Trantino.

For good measure, I downed a short glass of the Trantini Rosso, then sampled a few more wines before taking my leave of Giovanni. He waved away the euros I held out to pay for the wine, a gesture without words that clearly communicated that he wouldn't think of charging the capo from the Castello dei Trantini.

I visited a few more *enoteche* in Montalcino, asking most of the same questions and getting very similar answers.

When I checked my watch, I saw that it was nearing six o'clock. I needed to get back to the villa if I was going to shower and change for my date with Ilsa.

Dining Out in Montevarchi

I knew there wasn't a restaurant in nearby Pianella, at least none that I would bring Ilsa to. And I didn't want to drive as far as Siena or Radda, but I knew of a pleasant, out-of-the-way trattoria in Montevarchi just up the road from Castello dei Trantini. They served amazing pasta and grilled Tuscan meat, but more importantly, the place would provide a certain amount of privacy.

Privacy. I mulled the thought over. Was I looking for privacy because I didn't want too many people to recognize me taking an employee out to dinner? It was the better reason, but I knew I was really looking for the kind of dark-corner privacy that lent itself to my other instincts.

I arrived at Ilsa's home at eight o'clock sharp, cringing for a second when I remembered that no Italian arrives anywhere on time, but I pulled the Maserati to a stop and got out. She lived at home with her parents, although she was twenty-six years old, because in this country, the children — especially the young women   didn't usually move out until they were married.

The sun had just set but left the burnished glow on the horizon behind Ilsa's house. The air was beginning to cool and the occasional whisper of a breeze would ruffle the leaves of the olive trees next to the building. The house itself was made of stone, as usual in Tuscany, with broad beams that supported the roof protruding from between mortar and stone near the top of the second story. Several large pots adorned the narrow patio in front of the house, each heaped with flowers that were still aromatic at this time of the evening.

I strode up to the door, rapped my knuckles quickly on the solid wooden frame, and waited. Instead of being greeted by the sound of the door opening, a friendly "ciao" hailed me from above. I looked up to see Ilsa leaning out the second-story window, with a broad smile on her face. Thoughts of a Marcello Mastroianni film danced through my head as I admired her appearance in the window. She was wearing a body-hugging white halter-top with only thin straps to hold it in place. Her hair was a luxuriant golden color, brilliant and seemingly on fire from the backlighting in the window, and her skin glowed with the olive and bronze tones of a woman who spends much time outdoors — perhaps in my vineyards. The thought gave me a certain pleasure.

The shutters quickly closed, and I waited only a moment before the door swung open before me. Ilsa stood there, one hand still on the door, her weight shifted insouciantly onto one foot, the other hand resting on her hip.

"But, Signor Filippo, it's early, and I'm not ready yet." She said it in a most teasing tone, happy that I could see her "not ready yet," but chiding me for not observing the Italian custom of lateness.

"I'm sorry," I said, playing along with her. "Should I go and come back?"

"Of course not," she said with a laugh. She grabbed me by the elbow, pulled me inside the door, and shut it behind her.

There was no one else in evidence, and I wondered where her mother and father were. Ilsa explained that they had gone out to dinner, and she grinned impishly as she told me she had to convince her father that it was alright for him to be gone when I arrived. As she looked up at me past down-turned eyelashes, I realized that her father didn't feel a need to greet the "capo" from Castello dei Trantini, but that he needed to be there whenever a man — any man — arrived to see his daughter. I stifled an involuntarily gulp as I remembered that I was in Italy now, not the United States, and the rules of engagement would be different.

It's not that the Italians aren't romantic, quite the opposite. And the sometimes animal-hunger that attends their courting is probably the reason Italian culture has included such strict protections for its young women. From early teen years, and usually into very old age, Italian men and women possess a strong and healthy sexuality. It's in their music, their food, their clothes, and — as I stared at Ilsa, I realized — in their flirting. She let me have that moment to stare, to take her in, and then she was off to finish "getting ready."

As she walked back toward the steps to ascend to the upstairs bedroom, I had a chance to observe the rest of her wardrobe for the evening. The white halter-top displayed her tanned back, which was visible as she walked away. Below the halter-top she wore a tight black skirt, short enough to reveal a generous portion of her thighs, and on her feet she wore high heels that were each held in place by a single narrow strap from heel to toe.

Breathing in the scent of perfume she left in her wake, I couldn't imagine what was left to "getting ready."

I wandered through the parlor looking at the paintings on the walls, the shrine to the Virgin Mary in the corner, and the comfortable furnishings. It appeared that the Cantorini family was financially secure, but not affluent.

After waiting a few more moments, Ilsa reappeared. She looked as good as before, and I couldn't detect any change, so I wrote it off to female prerogative. She threw one of her brilliant smiles at me, grabbed a large scarf off the rack near the door, and invited me to exit.

The air had cooled still more, justifying Ilsa's decision to bring a wrap. Although Italy is warm, this was September and, in the countryside, the night air cooled off the day's heat, adding a freshness to the evening that was welcome after the day's labor.

I started for the passenger side of the car but Ilsa reached it first, pulling on the handle and letting herself in without so much as a sideways glance. She was clear about her independence, in an American sort of way, but she did it with a certain obviousness so that I would notice. I swung around the other side, slipped into the driver's seat, and we were off.

The owners of the trattoria I'd chosen, Álbero Verde, knew Nonno Filippo and served our wines. They didn't know me by sight but recognized my name when I called for a reservation. When we showed up at their door, Aldo and Mira were all smiles, mixing in comments of sympathy at Nonno's passing, but nonetheless pleased that the Trantino family members were still customers of their restaurant.

Ilsa was seated first, thanks to the deft movements of Aldo as he vied with his wife for the pleasure, and I sat next to her at the table in the corner. It was just the type of darkened corner I had hoped for. The proprietors then quickly backed away toward the kitchen, Mira handing a not-too-subtle rebuke to her errant husband for favoring the pretty girl at my table.

"Signor Filippo," Ilsa began, but I cut her off.

"*Per favore*, Ilsa, please, at least call me Filippo, if not Phil as my American friends do. I can't be '*signore*' to you while we are sitting together in this wonderful little restaurant."

Her smile combined both girlish innocence and a mature woman's enticement at my approach, and the total effect was very alluring.

"*Certo, signore*…oh, I'm sorry, Filippo," she said almost with a giggle. "Your friends call you Phil? What does that mean?"

"Filippo, of course," I said with a shrug of my shoulders. "It's just the American version of Filippo. It doesn't mean anything."

"Well, that won't do. I'll call you Filippo." Ilsa said this with confidence and comfort, waving the thought away, as if she was well trained in discarding translations that didn't fit some useful purpose.

"Filippo," she said, gently laying her hand on mine, "we haven't had time to speak seriously yet, but I want you to know how much I miss your nonno." The warmth of her skin sent a small bolt of electricity straight up my arm. "He was a wonderful man, an honest man, who worked as hard as his employees and never forgot one of us. His death has affected us all, and I will miss him greatly."

I was touched by the depth of her compassion, yet still excited by her touch. She clearly knew the effect of both and wanted both feelings to reach me. In another moment, she patted my hand with friendly affection, then switched her mood to one of gaiety.

"But we want to have fun tonight, *si*? Tell me, why do you like this place?"

Our conversation ranged far and wide as we sampled the many wonderful dishes of Álbero Verde. We talked about our families, how mine had moved to America, my bookstore back home, and how Tuscany had changed over the years — and yet still remained the same. We compared our ages — she rolled her eyes and feigned shock that I was "so" much older than her although we both knew the years between us meant little.

"I like working at the Castello," Ilsa said, "but I don't know if I want to stay there forever." Realizing that her English might not have been good enough to convey the proper message, she repeated it. "Oh, I like it very much," she said quickly, "but I think there are other things for me out there. And sooner or later, I'll get married and have children."

"What about going to school?" I asked.

"I attended the university and got my degree in botany, and Signor Basilio often gives me work to do in the vineyard. In time, he says, I should be able to become a vineyard manager, maybe for the Castello dei Trantini." This last bit she said with a twinkle in her eye.

Turning her attention on me, she said, "And of course, you are staying here now, to be the Castello's new capo, yes?"

I took some time to explain how that seemed the logical choice and it was, of course, very enticing, but I still couldn't decide how to manage the re-emigration to Italy. I mythologized my earlier life here in Tuscany and, for years, I would have sold my soul for a chance to move back. But now, with everything laid out for me, I couldn't decide whether it was the right path.

I probably ruminated on that subject too long, because I felt like I was merely giving voice to my own inner debate on the matter, but I saw that Ilsa was patiently listening to all my "maybes" and "ifs" and "why nots." Her dazzling smile never left her face, eyes sparkling when I related some favorite memory of mine, and she interjected pointed comments and thoughtful questions throughout, at times laughing at my indecision.

"So, do you remember me?" she asked suddenly.

"Well, yes," I began, "Of course, I do." But my slowness in responding gave her doubt.

"No, you don't," she chided me with a gentle wag of her index finger.

Remember her? I couldn't admit to her how much of an impression she always made, the most beautiful woman at the estate, and in all of Castelnuovo Berardenga.

As I pondered what to say, I think she was actually reading my mind, or she had noticed me in early times regarding her from a distance. At that moment, in Álbero Verde, I realized that our evening together had been planned long ago.

We spent a couple hours sampling the best dishes Aldo and Mira had to offer and we talked into the night. I got over my wariness about dating an employee and began to appreciate Ilsa in a different light. She was coquettish like any young Italian woman, yet seductive like their older sisters. She was intelligent enough to understand my dilemma, but playful enough to chide me for not wanting to stay with the family, her family the Cantorinis, and beautiful Tuscany.

After we finished dinner, we walked between the rows of the adjoining vineyard for a while. The moon was bright and the air sweet, and the scent of ripe grapes on the vine brought back many memories. We circled back to the car, settled into positions that were now comfortably closer together, and drove in near silence back to Ilsa's home.

When we arrived, lights shined through some of the lower and upper story windows and there was enough noise from inside to prove that her parents were already there. Before opening the door, as if she knew that would end everything, Ilsa leaned toward me and laid a soft kiss on my cheek. Her perfume, so near to me all night, was now attached to my skin and I enjoyed the presence of it on the quiet ride back to my villa on the hill.

Back at the Winery

"Signor Filippo, I'm so glad you're here, but you really must stay out of the way."

It was Vito, and he was scurrying about in his usual way, directing traffic in and out of the winery with flailing arms. His short stature failed to disguise his barrel-chested strength, and his energy — even in his early-seventies — would surpass that of most of the winery employees. His long sleeves were rolled up above his elbows so his arms wouldn't be restrained as he moved this bucket, then that hose. He was balding, it was true, but he had a tuft of sweaty gray hair that swung back and forth on his pate as he moved about the trucks and gondolas, the tanker-sized troughs that brought the grapes from the field to the winery.

I stood to the side and watched in amazement and appreciation for a few moments. Vito had managed the operation of the winery for many, many years, always treating it as if it were his own. He took great pride in the wine we produced, studiously avoiding releasing any that he considered less than the best. Nonno Filippo had always spoken highly of him, and although the winemakers had come from the Trantino family for generations, promoting Vito to the position was a masterstroke and one that served the Castello dei Trantini wines well.

I couldn't even remember when Vito was hired. It was well before I was born, I knew, but I could not remember anyone talking about how many years he had worked here. He just seemed to be a part of the whole scene, an indefatigable life force, always moving about, as if the winery without Vito would not have been the winery it was.

I watched as the trucks heavily laden with newly picked grapes arrived at the door of the winery. Each one dumped its load into an open-topped vat, to fall onto the auger below that turned and pushed the grapes up a chute to the crusher.

The crusher did just that: it crushed the grapes, but not crudely or with too great pressure. The secret of making fine wine was gentle treatment of the grapes and the juice. To begin the process, the crusher should be careful not to maul the fruit and release too much of the acids from the grape seeds, and mangle the stems so that their tart juices would mingle with those of the sweet grapes.

The crusher dropped the pulp into another chamber below. Here, the stems were separated from the skins and pulp, another step important to producing a softer wine, and then the skins and pulp, now called must, was delivered by a network of pipes and troughs to the fermenting vats.

The winery used gravity to transfer the fermenting juice in each stage of the process, but to get it started in fermentation, the must needed to be first pumped up into the waiting fermenters. The pumping was accomplished with powerful motors, but when so much volume was involved, and so many machines moving at once, this step in the process still required much human labor. Vito discouraged Nonno Filippo from automating this step even more, as had been done in many wineries throughout Europe, saying that it was only done once a year, and the work was good for the men.

There were twelve vats in this part of the winery, each holding five-hundred gallons of the pulp and skin mixture of newly crushed grapes. Three of the vats had already been filled, and the stirrings of initial fermentation could be faintly detected in the odor emanating from them.

As the truck pulled away from the crusher, Vito rushed past me once again, but stopped and came back. Quickly wiping his forehead with a sleeve stained by grapes, he looked up at me.

"Signor Filippo, I would like to talk to you more, but there is much work to do and the grapes are not as patient as you. Please," and with that he rushed off to wave at another truck pulling up to the entrance to the winery.

I walked up the long, twisting road to the Castello, past the osteria that served simple food to tourists and, on occasion, a winery worker with too much money to spend, past the small buildings that stored the heavy equipment used by the caretakers who tended the Castello grounds, and through the heavy iron gate that separated this walled oasis from the rest of the world.

Striding up the stairs to the wine library overlooking the vineyards, I sat glumly at the table Nonno Filippo used for his wine tastings. It was not quite four o'clock, the time Nonno conducted his daily ritual of tasting in this room, and my mind wandered back to him. A winery worker, Beppo, peeked carefully around the edge of the still-open door. He didn't say a word, but when I noticed him, he nodded then asked if I wanted to taste wines today. I couldn't suppress a smile, though for just a moment, then nodded yes, I would like to taste some wines today.

While waiting for him to return, I thought about Santo and Rita and my assignment. They had asked me to help them solve a murder, and so far, I had not uncovered any facts that would even suggest that murder had been committed. I agreed with their assessment, but Mirelli's comments stuck in my mind. If no one would want to kill Nonno Filippo, why should we assume that someone actually did? I was a bookseller, not a detective. I didn't even stock many mysteries in my bookstore at home because I had never been that interested in reading them myself.

Beppo, a nickname for Giuseppe, returned with eight bottles of wine. We talked a bit and I found out that he has worked at the Castello dei Trantini for about twelve years, first in the fields, then in the winery as Vito's assistant, then, lately, in the lab where the fruit was analyzed for sugar content, levels of tannic and malic acidity, and ripeness. Beppo has been responsible for setting up Nonno Filippo's daily tastings for the last few years and missed his chores only when he was on holiday with his family.

"Did you set up the bottles on the day Nonno Filippo died?" I asked.

"*Sì, signore.*"

The next questions were obvious.

"Was Nonno Filippo already in the room when you brought the wine in?"

"Oh, no, signore. I'm supposed to set up the wine before he arrives. But," he said looking sheepishly at me for the first time, "he's not usually here until four o'clock," no doubt referring to my early arrival.

"*Mi scusi,* Beppo," I said in apology, "I was not here for the tasting. I just was wandering the Castello and ended up here."

"*Grazie,*" he said while nodding his head, satisfied now that the ritual would resume without changing the time. He seemed genuinely relieved that this part of his day would remain the same.

"Did you notice anything unusual about the room on that day?"

"*No,* signore."

"Was there any dirt on the rug when you entered?"

"*No, signore.*"

"Was there any when you left?" I felt guilty asking this question, but I needed to know.

Beppo seemed to understand that I needed to ask, but he was still put off by the query.

"*No.*" This he said with finality, but with respect.

"*Grazie,* Beppo." And with that final comment, he left, closing the door behind him, and I turned to the bottles on the table.

An Afternoon's Work

Beppo had selected eight wines for me to taste. I knew a bit about Nonno Filippo's afternoon tastings, from stories told and from my surreptitious surveillance from the closet in the corner of the room, but this was the first time that the bottles were arranged for me.

Nonno Filippo used this time of the day to learn about wine, something he had done assiduously all his life. The eight wines were always selected in groups, always with something in common, but they could come from anywhere in the world. My grandfather used the time to compare the styles and analyze how the same grapes or blends could yield such different results, depending on where they were grown, the microclimate, winemaking strategies, and other factors. Today, all the wines displayed on the tasting table were based on the Sangiovese grape and, as if to make me feel at home on my first try at this routine, Beppo had selected all Tuscan wines.

Sangiovese has been grown in this region for centuries and it is responsible for many great wines, among them the perennial favorite — Chianti. The formula for Chianti was developed by Baron Bettino Ricasoli, the nineteenth-century lord of the Castello di Brolio. He also happened to be the first prime minister of Italy following its unification in the 1860s. His descendants still owned the property — the estate has been in the Ricasoli family since 1141 A.D. — and they still make world-famous wine from the vineyards surrounding the castle.

Sangiovese is also responsible for many other non-Chianti wines. There is, of course, Brunello di Montalcino, one of the most expensive wines in all of Italy. There's also a host of so-called Super Tuscans — wines loosely based on Sangiovese, cabernet sauvignon, and other "foreign" grapes — blends winemakers believed were so good they didn't need to comply with the Italian government's restrictive laws in order to qualify for the moniker of Chianti.

The little grape is also the base for other, less well-known wines, but still popular and very good indeed. I gazed at the labels and saw that it was a hodge-podge of Sangiovese that Beppo had chosen for me that day. There were two bottles of Morellino di Scansano, a rich, ripe full-bodied red from the Maremma, a popular region of western Tuscany; three bottles of Sangiovese di Toscana from different properties; and two other Tuscan blends that included Sangiovese as the main component. Apparently just for fun, or perhaps to use as a benchmark, Beppo sneaked in a Sangiovese from Umbria, the region bordering Tuscany on the east.

All the corks were pulled but remained in the neck of the bottle. A simple, clear glass was positioned in front of each bottle, and a pad and pen were left at one end of the table, with the wines already listed on the top sheet of paper, including descriptions of the wines' origins, grape percentages, production levels, and approximate market price. There was no attempt to hide the identity of the bottles — this was not to be a blind tasting. Nonno Filippo's goal at these afternoon tastings was to learn about the wines, not judge them, and he wanted as much information as possible at his fingertips to enhance the learning process. Beppo made certain that I would have the same advantage, and thanks to the comfort of routine, he didn't feel that it was important to ask whether I agreed.

I pulled the cork from both Morellino wines and poured a small sample of each into nearby glasses. Then, lifting one glass in each hand, I walked to the window to take advantage of the afternoon sunlight streaming into the room. The wines were both remarkably deep purple-red, a sign of youth but also a sign of depth and concentration.

I stuck my nose into the first glass, inhaled deeply, then withdrew it and repeated the action with the second wine. The first was very fruity and floral, with focused aromas of blackberry and toast, and a whiff of dust and earth for good measure. The second glass yielded a bouquet of rose petals, tobacco, black cherry and wet earth. Breathing deeply and examining both wines again in the window light, I took a mouthful of the first wine. It tasted like it smelled, but with slowly evolving layers of fruit, separating themselves into black cherry, raspberry, leather, and pipe tobacco. The second wine was less complex, favoring simple fruit flavors delicately balanced against accents of wet earth and mushrooms.

In this way, I worked my way around the table, tasting the wines in pairs or triplets, depending on the styles available, but always comparing each wine to something else. At one moment, with my nose plunged deep into a glass, I paused and smiled as I thought of my grandfather. This was what he did every day; this was his passion, and he would be standing here now tasting these very wines if he was still alive. The thought pained me a bit, but I was acclimating myself to the new arrangement, and I smiled at the thought that I was taking his place, that this was now going to be my routine. Catching myself in mid-reverie, I invoked a silent caution: I had not yet decided whether I was staying in Tuscany, and frankly didn't know what I was going to do.

"Don't go too fast," I muttered aloud, to no one but myself, a caution that applied to tasting wine as well as sampling the other pleasures of life.

Alimentàrio

There's a little store in Pianella that sells everything a little house would need, from cleaning supplies and newspapers to fresh fruits and wine. Salame and aged pecorino compete for space on the too-small butcher's table at the end of the checkout counter, and dried goods like rice and pasta are stacked right next to the candy display. And if the preference for *legume*, *pesce*, and *gelato* weren't apt reminders of the country you were visiting, the television in the corner with its non-stop coverage of the latest soccer games would be.

It was this *alimentàrio*, roughly equivalent to a general store in America, I thought of the next morning when I realized I was running low on the supplies that Elisabetta had left for me on her second visit to the villa.

Pianella was near enough to the Castello, and I knew I could make a quick run down there before a midday meeting with an old friend, so I shut the door to the villa, stepped quickly down to the Maserati that I now parked in front of the villa instead of leaving with Riccardo at the garage, and backed away from the low stone wall that separated my little home from the vineyards below.

I drove down the dirt lane toward the Castello, and then swung a sharp left turn around a field house sporting a wall shrine to the Virgin Mary, to follow another dirt road that would take me off the estate and towards my destination. I was clearly enjoying my stay in Tuscany at that point, more than I expected to. No doubt the dates I'd had with

Ilsa played a major role in my newfound pleasures, but being home at Castello dei Trantini had a rejuvenating effect on me. I had always loved this place, the azure blue skies, the scent of grapes and rosemary drifting on the breeze, even the dust that wafted behind the car as I sped down the parched roads.

Nonno Filippo's death was a specter that I couldn't put entirely from my mind, and each time the thought crept back into my consciousness, I shuddered. He was a vibrant life force, a man of pleasure and of strong emotion, someone not easily forgotten by even a casual stranger. As his grandson and namesake, I knew I would never be able to forget him, and somber thoughts clouded my mind as I pulled to a sudden halt on the curb in front of the *alimentàrio*. I turned off the motor and sat in silence for a moment. I wasn't over the pain of losing him, and I didn't want to forget that this life, this place, the Castello and all of its environs were really what he gave to me. I was in Tuscany now and, no matter where I lived my life, my heart would always be in Tuscany because he gave me this.

After a moment of reflection, and recognizing that I would have to continue with the daily chores — not to mention carry on with my life — I stepped out of the car to the stares of some local townspeople who were probably wondering why this young man was sitting in this too-rich car, staring down at the floorboards. I smiled and stepped through the *alimentàrio's* front door.

Once inside, the buzz of activity in the shop replaced the pastoral quiet of the rural outside. There were only about seven or eight customers, helped by the husband and wife who owned the place, but Italians talk loud and almost every conversation is spoken with the gusto of an argument. The television blared the play-by-play of the Trapani-Bari soccer game, and even the opening and closing of doors on the refrigerated bins sounded louder than usual.

Friends had always asked me why Italian restaurants were louder than other restaurants, even in the States. It was partly because of the hard surfaces, I told them, the stone floors, solid walls not softened by fabric coverings, and so on, but it was also the Italians themselves.

Italians didn't love noise, but they embraced it as a sign of life. Waving hands and locking stares during heated conversations were part of the same thing, constant reminders that there is blood coursing through their veins. At the end of the day, with all that noise, all that hand waving, all that emotion packed into every action, the Italians were tired. They slept deeply, perhaps exhausted from all the activity of the day, and — I believe — because they think that sleeping is just as serious as any other activity and, if they're going to do it, they're going to do it with gusto!

The *alimentàrio* reflected that basic premise about life in Italy. A pleasant "*buon giorno*" greeted me when I entered, followed by a quick look from the proprietor while he sliced some pepperoni for a customer. I grabbed a basket and started to load it with the essentials, bread, oil, pasta, some fresh tomatoes, and even fresher mozzarella from the refrigerator. I didn't need wine, of course, and there was an herb garden just outside the door to the villa, so I passed up the luscious-looking basil I saw on the counter. A hunk of Parmigiano Reggiano, some truffle oil, cartons of orange juice and milk, a brick of ground coffee for the espresso machine, and I approached the counter for the meat I would need to keep me going for a few days.

I looked up as I neared the line of three customers and saw Elisabetta standing there. We exchanged a quick glance, looked at the baskets each of us was holding, and both of us started to laugh. We had selected mostly the same things and, knowing how well she had taken care of me, I had a suspicion that we were both there shopping for the same person.

"*Buon giorno, Signor Filippo,*" she said.

"*Buon giorno, signora. Per chi compri?*" I asked, knowing already the answer was she buying for me.

With a laugh, she answered, "*Per lui,*" pointing to me and my basket.

Elisabetta was about twenty years older than me and very attractive. She had thick, tousled black hair that she showed little interest in reigning in. Her clothes were proper, but not conservative, and she enjoyed showing off her tanned and ample breasts with blouses that dipped low enough to reveal them. Her hips showed that she had borne children, but the loose skirt that hung from them made her mid-section and legs look stunning. Her face was bright with homespun happiness, and her eyes shined when she smiled. Despite our age differences, she was a woman who could lead a man into mischief.

"*Perche?*" she asked simply.

"What do you mean, what?" I replied, a little confused.

"Why are you shopping? Aren't I taking good enough care of you," she asked with a sideways glance and a pout.

I didn't know how to respond. Certainly she was taking care of me, but I wasn't her responsibility. I tried to explain that. She put a hand up in front of her and said, "No, no, no. You are the capo, and I work at the Castello. You *are* my responsibility."

Then with a conspiratorial wink, she told me that she had this same discussion with Anita the other day and the two had an understandable disagreement on the subject. Anita had taken care of Nonno Filippo and thought she would carry on that responsibility with me, especially in light of the conversation I had with her. But the villa was Elisabetta's charge, and she was shopping for "Signor Filippo," she told Anita, planting her fists on her hips as she told me, as I'm sure she did when she said it to Anita.

Then she laughed. She said her argument with Anita seemed so funny, but though she laughed at it Anita hadn't. Since then, they came to an agreement that Elisabetta would continue to stock food in the villa and Anita would buy for the Castello, and each would be responsible for restocking as I and my guests consumed the food. "*D'accordo,*" they agreed behind fixed stares.

Just as she finished her recap of the tussle with Anita, Elisabetta reached out and took my basket from me.

"I'll take that," she said with authority, graced with a flirtatious smile. She left no doubt that she intended to take care of my kitchen needs. Funny, I thought, how her look let me know she knew more than I could imagine, including a subtle inference that she knew about

Ilsa, and the fact that we'd been seeing more of each other in the last few days.

Renewing Old Friendships

When my morning's chores suddenly evaporated, I had time to kill before *pranzo*, the midday meal. I decided to take a leisurely drive around the property to get reacquainted with the vineyards, but first I would have to trade in the Maserati for a more "sensible" farm automobile.

"It's a good thing you brought that back," said Riccardo, after I had pulled up to the garage and explained my purpose. "I certainly wouldn't want you driving such a beautiful car around through the hills and brush in the vineyards. Besides I should look it over, check the car's vital signs, and clean it up a bit."

I think Riccardo simply missed having the Maserati in his care, but I wouldn't begrudge him some time with *la macchina*. This wonderful tribute to Italian engineering had been my companion through my re-immersion into Tuscan life, and I was anxious to have it back, but I could be patient.

"*Ecco,*" he said, "here, you can use this one."

He was holding out the keys to another car and, when I saw what he was pointing at I laughed. Not because the choice was not good, but because he was pointing at the Fiat that Santo had originally suggested I drive while staying at the Castello. Riccardo quickly got my meaning, and a broad smile stretched across his face.

So, Santo had meant for me to drive the "sensible" car. Perhaps it was just a small sign of his disappointment that an American — even one that was his cousin — had come to assume a position of authority at the Castello.

I drove around the garage and quickly dove headlong into the vineyards. Here, the vines were strong and tall, some of them already picked but some rows had yet survived the pickers' shears. The taut wires stretching from post to post down the long rows shouldered a mantle of dark green leaves that were just then beginning to show the burnt orange and tawny yellow colors of fall.

The rows were arranged in parallel lines, marching up the hills and disappearing over the summit like an endless parade of soldiers. Every so often, there was a break in the rows, a lane slightly wider than the usual six-foot spacing, to allow large farm equipment access to the various regions of the vineyard. At one of these lanes, I turned right, bouncing in my seat as the Fiat's old shocks absorbed too little of the terrain, instead transferring it along to my body's own shock absorbers. The lane was rutted and scored by asymmetric lines where erosion had gotten the better of the earth. Wild grass mingled with the outcropping of solid rock poking up from beneath the surface, and bees and other winged insects marked the silence with their sounds.

I stopped the car and got out, feeling the warm morning sun on my shoulders and bare arms, and walked closer to the vines. Here there were still more grapes to pick, and as I leaned toward a vine heavy with its fruit, I smelled the sweet fragrance of ripe grapes. Wine grapes were harvested much sweeter than table grapes, about twice the sugar level, and the aromas were sometimes overpowering. Cradling a bunch of dark red grapes in my hands, I lifted it up and put my nose in among the berries, inhaled deeply and imagined how good the juice was going to be as wine.

The grass underfoot was prickly and dry, a good sign for harvest. Water was important for the fruit, but the best water came from deep in the ground. For this reason, vines planted in poor, rocky soil usually reached deep into the earth for sustenance, and as a result drank the cleanest water available. Rainwater would help the vines, but it had yet to benefit from the natural filtration offered by passing through the layers of the earth. And in the fall, when harvest was near, rainwater would be absorbed right through the skins of the grapes, plumping them up too much and watering down the pulp inside. Therefore, a dry harvest season was the best and vignerons prayed for no rain — and certainly no storms — in the weeks just before the pickers arrived.

I was lost in thought as I heard someone call out my name. I looked up, then to the right and left, and still couldn't find the source of the voice. I heard my name one more time, but from behind me, so I turned and saw Rita coming down the lane. It was rare to find Rita in the vineyard; her office was in Siena, and when she did visit the Castello, it was usually to see Santo.

"Ciao, Filippo. Are you lost?" she said with a laugh.

"*No, cara,* I'm just enjoying a morning in the vineyard."

"Perhaps you'd like to join the pickers when they come through here during harvest?" I knew she was ribbing me, because we both knew how hard the pickers' work was. It may be romanticized in the movies, but it's back-breaking work in the hot sun, and the men and women who work the vineyards do so only because they have few other choices. They're good at what they do, and so they should be considered skilled labor, but most of them would happily exchange that skill for something with less physical labor.

"No, no," I looked down and laughed a little, "I don't think they need my help. But I like being here. I like seeing the grapes while they're still hanging from the vines, before they disappear into the pickers' baskets."

"And before they disappear into the fermentation vats?"

"That part," I said with more excitement, "that part I like! And yes, before, you ask, I will be around for that. But why are you here?"

"I wanted to deliver some papers for Anita that dealt with Nonno Filippo's accounts in Siena. Not his wine accounts, mostly bank statements, miscellaneous papers. But while I was there, Anita told me she got a call from a friend of yours? A man named Roberto?"

"Yes, yes," I said and quickly checked my watch for the time. I got so involved in tooling around the vineyard that I had lost track of the time. It was already 1:00, the time I was supposed to meet Roberto at the osteria on the property.

"Rita," I said as I made my way quickly back to the car. "I must go; I'm late for my lunch. Can I drop you somewhere?"

"What, you think I walked here? No, I have my own car," she said with a chuckle, waving me away as I raced to my car.

I walked briskly to the Fiat. It had a light coating of dust from its day in the vineyard and as I settled into the seat I looked over at the Alpha Romeo that Rita was driving. Her car was jet black with cream-colored interior and looked so elegant that dust wouldn't have dared to settle on it. I pulled away with a wave back to Rita and regretted that I wouldn't have time to change into fresher clothes — or a better car.

Roberto Vitale was a friend from my childhood. He lived in nearby Castelnuovo Berardenga, but within the town limits, not on the outskirts as we did at the Castello. We met at the elementary school I attended before emigrating to the United States and, in those early years of childhood, we spent many afternoons together playing at the Castello or the playground near his home. Since leaving for America, Roberto and I stayed in touch by letter and occasionally would get a chance to visit on my trips back to Tuscany, but our relationship had changed. We were both adults now, into our thirties, he with a wife and family, me still single and living a life very different from the one I lived when in Italy.

But Roberto and I still saw eye to eye on a lot of things. The shared past seemed to give us an excuse to discuss things honestly, and I knew an afternoon with him would bring laughter as well as thoughtful rumination. He was not associated with the Castello, but he lived nearby and the Trantino family and the Castello dei Trantini were an important part of the local community, so he would be expected to know a good bit about the events taking place here.

"Ciao, Filippo!" Roberto stood from the table and waved heartily as he saw me pull to a stop beside the osteria. As he approached he cast a glance at the dusty old Fiat, gave me a bear hug, then made fun of the car I was driving.

"So, I thought you'd be driving a nice expensive car, being the new head of the Castello dei Trantini, but perhaps times aren't so good, eh?" He said this with a slap on my arm.

"No, actually, this isn't the car I usually drive," but the skeptical look on his face led me to conclude that he wouldn't believe whatever I was about to tell him, so my voice trailed off.

We sat at the table under the pergola, shaded from the afternoon sun by the vines that meandered across the latticework above our heads. The osteria was perched on a small flat terrace of land alongside the road leading up to the Castello, surrounded by tall cypress and the arching branches of taller oaks. Here, the air was cooled by the altitude, and from the gentle breeze that wafted up from the valley through the trees and forest.

Roberto hailed the waitress and she came with a basket of bread and another glass to add to the one he had already filled from the carafe of red wine on the table. Pouring a healthy amount into my glass, he raised his in salute; we clinked the solid glass tumblers of wine and drank the lightly chilled liquid inside.

Red wine was too often served warm, and often taken too seriously by Americans. Most Europeans appreciated their wine cooler, not quite refrigerated, but the temperature of an old cellar. And Italians appreciated simple wines as often as the much-talked-about world-class wines that came from their vineyards. Wine was a way of life in Italy, a necessary accouterment to every meal, and most of the people I knew in Tuscany didn't spend the first five minutes of every dinner talking about the wine — they just drank it and appreciated it.

"So, how's the Castello, Filippo?" he asked. "I'm very sorry to hear about your grandfather. He was a great man."

"Yes, everyone agrees. It's a sad loss. I'm still getting used to the idea that my trips home won't find him at the gate waiting for me with that big smile on his face."

"Well, these 'trips home' as you call them," Roberto noted with a shrug, "perhaps this is home now, yes?"

I looked down into the tumbler of wine, searching for the answer I'd been contemplating since I'd arrived in Italy. "Yes, I suppose that's possible, but I find it harder to decide now than I ever thought it would be."

"You are the new capo, the one to take over the reins of the estate. The one to manage the property for the family, isn't this true?"

"Yes, that's what is expected. The property passes down to the first grandson, the first son's first son. That's me," I said still pondering the shapeless reflections in the glass. "I never quite understood that," I added, "why the estate passed on to the grandson, not the son."

With a shrug of his shoulders, Roberto attempted an informed opinion on the question. "Well, in Italy, of course, the names pass on that way too. Perhaps the tradition was started at the Castello dei Trantini so that *il proprietare* would always be named Filippo?" He said this with raised eyebrows, and cocked his head to the side as if this position would lend the comment more credibility.

"What do the people in town say about Nonno Filippo?" I asked him.

"That he was a great man, that he was generous and fair, that he was the 'first citizen' of Castelnuovo Berardenga."

"No, that's not what I meant." As I said this, Roberto's face turned to one of concern and slight confusion. "Do people talk about my grandfather's death? How it happened."

Roberto paused to consider this, staring at me to glean more from my expression before answering, and took a long drink of wine before he spoke.

"Your grandfather fell out of the window on the second story of the Castello. He landed on the stone steps below. That's a long fall for an old man," he said, then added, "I'm sorry, but he *was* old." With this, Roberto lifted his glass in an unconscious salute to the man, a gesture so natural and fitting that his meaning was easily understood.

"Santo and Rita think that perhaps Nonno Filippo was murdered."

Roberto was too wise to have been taken by surprise by my statement, but he still paused before responding.

"Yes," he began, "I've heard this."

"From who?"

"No one, actually. Truly, no one. I can't think of where the comment comes from and I also don't put too much stock in it."

"You mean you don't believe it?" I asked.

"I mean I don't think there's much reason to believe it. Who would want to kill your grandfather?"

"No one, from what we all know and have said, but the circumstances of his death are perplexing."

I didn't go into the details of how Nonno Filippo had fallen out of the window, didn't discuss the torn pants legs and the unfinished glass of wine on the windowsill. I waited for another moment to see if the silence would draw more out of Roberto.

"The talk has been that such a great man shouldn't have had to die such a terrible death. I think most of the townspeople just think there's something of the evil eye about how he met his end," Roberto said.

"Evil eye?" I knew the phrase and knew that Italians believed that someone could be jinxed by a foe, that a spell could be cast that would result in tragedy. It was one of a host of superstitions that Italians still cling to.

"Who would cast an evil eye on my grandfather?"

"Again, as I said, no one, and no one in town thinks so either. It's just the way he went." Roberto said this last thing with slumping shoulders, as if he didn't want to discuss my grandfather's demise any longer.

"Do you know Sergio Berconi?" he asked.

"I know the name, but I don't think I know the man."

"He's a good friend of your grandfather's. He lives in Montalcino now. Perhaps you should talk to him. Maybe he knows something about Nonno Filippo's life that you haven't found out yet."

I agreed and would look forward to another trip to Montalcino anyway. I decided I would get to that in the next day or two, but first Roberto and I would get to this meal the waitress had just delivered to the table.

The conversation switched to more agreeable subjects as we each took helpings of the grilled vegetables aromatically scented with sage and balsamic vinegar. Bread was torn off to sop up drops of the marinade that fell from the zucchini and eggplant appetizer, and wine was quaffed in greater quantities as our hunger ruled over our exchange of stories from the years gone by. The platter of grilled vegetables was soon replaced by great bowls of pasta. The steam from the bowls transported aromas of toasted pignoli and fresh herbs, and generous shavings of Parmigiano Reggiano topped the bowls.

When we had completed that course, the waitress brought out another platter, this one bearing rosemary chicken, roasted on a spit until it was so tender that it fell from the bone. The whole garlic cloves that had been tucked under the skin of the chicken were now roasted and sweet to the taste, and these we mashed and spread into the broth that ran from the meat. A side dish of sliced carrots and grilled pearl onions, with a sprinkling of celery seed and extra-virgin olive oil, was added to the table. All the while, we ate and talked, cheering our advance into adulthood, making salacious reference to our wild younger years, and Roberto regularly reminding me that I was still single and still eligible.

After the chicken was neatly picked clean and the platter rescued from our marauding by the waitress, she brought another carafe of wine, fresh figs and oranges the size of melons. We pried into each to devour the inner meat of the fruit, sipped the stark black espresso, and sipped more wine as we worked our way through a fine afternoon meal.

After the fruit, there was dessert — a dark chocolate cake with fresh strawberries and cream — and when that was gone, there was more bread and more wine. The meal stretched on into the afternoon.

A Quiet Evening

I returned to the villa after my long visit with Roberto and sat in the shade of the loggia for a while. After the quantity of wine we'd consumed, I didn't need any more to keep me company, so I just sat there with my feet propped up on another chair, and leaned my chin into my hand resting elbow-down on the table.

The high heat of the afternoon had ebbed a bit as the hours wore on. It was around five o'clock when the workers began to trudge out of the fields and back to their old battered cars for the drive home, looking forward to the long, languishing supper and the short night's rest before beginning work again the next day. Thoughts of the harvest always brought the color out in everyone's cheeks, but the actual work was grueling and lasted for several weeks. At this time of the day, with their strength drained and thoughts of a shady spot to doze prominent in their minds, the enthusiasm for collecting grapes and making wine waned.

Vito clattered by in an old station wagon. He looked up at me in the loggia, waved briefly, but had a dissatisfied look on his face. I assumed he was unhappy with the progress of the grape picking, though the weather and seasonal conditions seemed perfect. I made a mental note to ask him about it later.

The hours slid by with me retaining my position at the table on the loggia. I made little change to my posture or situation, except that after a while I decided that another bit of wine wouldn't be so bad after all. As the day insects were being replaced by the evening bugs buzzing around the lantern I lit on the table, I settled back into my chair with a bottle of our Rosso di Montalcino from three years ago. Many people assume that red wine continues to taste better the older it gets. But those who truly know wine know that most of it has a short life. Although there are historic examples of wines continuing to improve for decades, including some wines from Tuscany, many of them — including the bottle I was cradling in my left hand — were best consumed young.

I lifted the short stubby glass to my mouth and sipped gently at first, noting the fresh fruit and earthy accents as the liquid slid across my tongue, then took another turn at the glass and poured a more generous gulp for my pleasure. The Rosso was a superb wine for a very fair price, and it provided the estate with a substantial amount of income through exportation to America and the rest of Europe.

As I contemplated the wine, I contemplated Nonno Filippo's life. My thoughts were on what he did while he was alive, who he was, and why he was so well loved, instead of thinking about how he died. He was a burly man, one who laughed with his entire body instead of just his mouth, a man who lived life every day. He would take advantage of situations — such as when Tuscany had a too-big harvest and he bought excess wine from other producers who couldn't handle the volume — but he wouldn't take advantage of people. Even in that year, when vineyardists were complaining that the crop was too big for their fermenters, he paid fair prices to relieve them of the tonnage of grapes, then turned them into bulk wine that he sold without a label to restaurants in the region.

Nonno Filippo was not so much interested in making wine as making memories. He seemed to consider himself lucky to have been born into his situation, and he wanted to use the glory of the Trantino estate to better the community. Perhaps this is why Roberto had referred to him as the "first citizen" of Castelnuovo Berardenga. My grandfather donated money to worthy causes, usually without allowing that the donations be publicized, but he also took over the responsibility of funding whole projects to improve the community. Electrification is not new to Italy, but sometimes reaching the areas lying too far from the city centers was difficult. Nonno Filippo had paid for the poles and power lines to bring electricity to the farms on the northern side of the city and then instituted reforms in the sanitation department and paid to have pipes laid along main roads leading out of town toward smaller communities. It turned out that many of his workers lived in these residential hubs outside the main part of Castelnuovo Berardenga, but no one objected when Nonno Filippo brought benefits to his employees first because others also gained from his generosity.

And the other members of the Trantino family didn't object either. Nonno Filippo didn't own the estate, we all did, and he was just *il proprietare*. But he was the patriarch of the family and the one who made all the decisions, about winemaking, money management, and community service. We drew benefits — and income — from the success of the estate and we enjoyed less tangible joys from his work. It would not be our place to question his decisions about how the Castello dei Trantini would fit into the community.

At this, I wondered how the rest of the Trantino family would feel if I did assume the patriarchal responsibilities and began — at the tender age of thirty-two — to make the broad decisions that fell upon the capo of the estate.

Draining the glass and pouring some more, I then thought about his death. There was something so medieval about falling from the heights of an old stone castle, crumpled up on the steps beside a hundred-year-old vineyard, and being found the next day in the sweet mist of the morning fog. Perhaps it was precisely this atmosphere and the thousand-year-old castello peering down at me from the hill that made the death seem macabre. Without any facts that suggested murder — except for those heard from Santo and Rita that still made me wonder — perhaps it was just the place, the time, and the antiquity of the Tuscan countryside that made mysteries out of unfortunate accidents.

Deep in my reverie, I heard the honk of a car. I stood up to look over the edge of the loggia's wall down toward the driveway below.

Ilsa was standing there beside her little blue car, resting against the door, with her right hand on the car's horn and a suggestive smile stitched across her lips.

"*Allora*," she began, "is there any wine up there for me?"

"Ah, and how could I not have wine for such an attractive woman?"

She looked around, over one shoulder then the other, and looked back at me with an accusing squint of her eyes. "Am I just the first one here, or would there be another woman?"

I cocked my head to the side and offered an almost apologetic smile. "That's not what I meant, but if you're still interested, I still have wine."

The game was over and Ilsa quickly bounded up the steps to the loggia. Before settling into the chair next to me, she wrapped her lithe arms around my neck, peered for a second into my eyes for effect, then closed her mouth on mine. I had already enjoyed as much from her in the courtship that had developed between us, but this left my knees weak. There was something about the kiss, both hungry and yet soothing, that I didn't know where to go next.

Ilsa settled the matter for me, releasing me as quickly as she had come, poured herself a glass of wine, and sat quickly into the chair with the best view of the valley. I was momentarily frozen in place, and as I shook out of my trance, I saw an impish smile take up residence on her face. Yes, indeed, she had gotten my attention and — yes — she was now drinking wine and not playing around anymore. Oh, how these women could control us, I thought with rueful pleasure.

We sipped and talked into the evening. When hunger crept upon us, Ilsa and I went into the kitchen to see what Elisabetta had brought for us to enjoy. When I saw the flowers on the table just inside the door, I silently thanked Elisabetta for brightening up the place in time for Ilsa's visit, but when I saw the jar of dill pickles in the refrigerator, I was confused. I wasn't a big fan of pickles, preferring the many kinds of olives that Italy had to offer, and I couldn't figure out why Elisabetta had decided to get this very-American condiment for my villa.

"Oh," cooed Ilsa looking over my shoulder, "I love those!" she added with excitement, then grabbed for the jar of pickles on the shelf in the refrigerator. I stood there with a dumb look on my face, staring at the other chilled items before me, realizing that Elisabetta was a bit more informed — and a lot more involved — than I had imagined.

We put together some pasta with a sauce of grilled Portobello mushrooms and sun-dried tomatoes, lubricated with a bit of the Castello's own olive oil. We added a large salad *a la Italiana,* as Ilsa called it, a mixture of fields greens, crumbled goat cheese, toasted pignoli, and kalamata olives, made all the more succulent with a combination of olive oil and a dash of aged balsamic vinegar. Grabbing each of the bowls, platters, and plates, we brought everything to the table on the loggia. Just before we sat down I ducked back inside to get another bottle of wine.

We ate slowly and a lot, drank deeply of the wine and each other's company, and watched the sun set on the far horizon. The sky turned from orange, to crimson, to purplish-black, and lights began to dot the skyline of ancient Siena off to the left.

Ilsa and I had spent more and more time together as my days in Tuscany had turned into weeks, but we never were alone as we were then. We had enjoyed lunches in town, and pleasant — though short — conversations at the winery while she was at work, but that evening gave us our first chance since that dinner at Álbero Verde to focus on each other without any interference from friends or strangers.

Ilsa talked often of her parents and laughed about her father's protective nature. Her mother was also concerned that their only daughter — and only child — be safe and secure, but she understood better than her husband how important it would be for Ilsa to find happiness through pleasure. It was the pleasure principle that made Ilsa's father pause. He agreed with the "happiness thing," as he called it, but it was that "pleasure thing" that worried him. Ilsa laughed as she told me this, and she said her mother had laughed at it too. They both knew what he meant, and Ilsa's father understood when her mother had tried to explain, patting his hand as if he was a child, that pleasure is an important part of a girl's happiness.

He waved away the thought, being fully aware of it but denying it at the same time, and changed the subject. That's the way it always went, Ilsa said, whenever they talked about how she would need to meet men to find one she would marry. "Then meet a man, and be happy," her father would say firmly, and with a wag of his index finger, "but not so much of that pleasure thing."

I couldn't help but laugh with her, although I felt a little guilty at the same time. I looked at Ilsa's bare legs below the hem of her peasant skirt, and how her breasts pushed against the fabric of her shirt and peeked slightly above the rim of the neckline. I looked at her golden hair, listened to her accented English pronunciation, and was intoxicated by the smell of her perfume. And I thought about her father's wagging finger and reproach about too much of that "pleasure thing." But when she looked up at me with those sparkling blue eyes, I could tell she had done it again. She had avoided my gaze just for a moment to give me a chance to admire her beauty, but then she was ready to accept my surrender. She looked up, our eyes gazed deep into each other's being, and I was lost.

Nothing tipped off the table, even though we both rose suddenly to wrap our bodies together, and nothing on the table was moved — not bottle, glass, or plate — until the next morning when we returned to clean up.

Morning with Anita

I woke early the next morning and made some espresso before venturing out into the vineyards for a little walking exercise. The talk with Roberto the day before re-energized me and I decided that I needed to make more progress in solving the mystery about my grandfather's death.

After several minutes of unconscious wandering around the estate, I found myself in front of a small hotel that stood incongruously in the middle of the Castello dei Trantini property. I couldn't quite understand why the Trantini family had let this establishment come to exist here. The building occupied by the hotel was already there on the property, had been on the property already for more than one-hundred years, and a businessman excited about the prospects of luring American tourists to vacation at one of Tuscany's great wine estates convinced the family that he should be able to convert the unused building into a hotel. A deal was reached in which the proprietor agreed to invest his own money in refurbishing the building and adjacent swimming pool, install a restaurant, and command the establishment rent-free for ten years. After that, the Trantini family would be able to decide whether he would have to go, or stay on under the same, or altered, financial arrangements.

I walked past the hotel and up the dirt road toward the Castello. The lane was shaded by a line of cypress trees on the right, and sloped off on the left into the bowl-shaped vineyard below. Passing by the vineyard I reached the Castello and entered through a side gate known only to family members, an entrance which saved us the necessity of accessing the property through the more public iron-gate entrance at the front of this hilltop fortress.

I went directly to the first-floor sitting room, opened the tall wide doors that led out onto the terrace, and sat down at the table in the room to gather my thoughts. In just a matter of moments, as if she already knew I was on the property, Anita appeared at the door, laid a basket of fruit on the table, and put a knife and a small plate in front of me. I told her I wasn't hungry, but she only smiled and walked out of the room. After a few minutes of drumming my fingers on the table, trying unsuccessfully to answers questions I didn't even know how to ask, I looked at the fruit and, choosing an apple from the basket, picked up the knife and started to peel it. Its juicy sweetness tasted good and made me forget my failed investigation, and I smiled as I realized that Anita probably knew this and that was why she brought the basket in. No wonder Nonno Filippo thought so much of her.

As I made my way through the apple, Anita reappeared with a tray filled with rolls hot from the oven, a small, two-chambered espresso pot steaming from the hot broth inside, and a small bowl of sugar cubes. Italians preferred to sweeten their espresso, a habit I lost when I moved to America, but I was beginning to go back to my old ways now that I was home again. I lifted the pot and poured a bit of the deep, black liquid, and the room filled with the aromas of dark roasted coffee beans. Then I plopped a sugar cube into the espresso cup, stirred it quickly, and drank it down in one gulp.

Italians like to consume their food sitting down, resting while they are eating. But they like their coffee on the run and, so, they have developed the habit of taking it in a single draught. This explains the multitude of coffee bars throughout the cities, stainless-steel counters with little room behind them for anything more than the barista and his espresso machine. With a deftness that comes only with repetition, he would yank the handle of the coffee basket to separate it from the machine, tap the basket quickly against the side of the cup holding used grounds, refill the basket with fresh coffee, and yank the basket back into place. With a turn of a knob and a jab at one of the buttons, the barista would then turn away and busy himself with other duties. It was a timely ritual that would bring him back to the espresso machine at precisely the moment when the tiny cups below the spout would be filled to capacity. A second too soon and he would have to wait impatiently for the cups to fill; a second too late and the precious liquid would be spilling onto the counter. In this way, coffee mavens throughout Italy delivered this life-sustaining beverage to anxious patrons, customers who stopped by only long enough for a caffeine fix and then hustle away to some other important assignation.

So, I poured another cup of espresso, added the sugar cube, and stirred it just long enough for the sugar to dissolve. Then I downed the small quantity of coffee in the cup and went to work on one of the rolls still steaming from the oven.

Anita stood sentinel while I began my breakfast, *la prima colazione.* The satisfied smile on her face held many meanings, and I considered my recent conversation with Elisabetta and decided that Anita's smile also conveyed a sense of victory for her. She was the one feeding me now, even if it was only breakfast.

"*Mangia,*" she encouraged, with hands lifting up in a gesture of offering. "*Mangia,*" she repeated, insisting that I eat more than one apple and one roll.

As I picked up another roll, I explained to her that I would be going to Siena that day to visit with the Cosco firm, the family that handled the export of wines from Castello dei Trantini.

"*Sì, signore,*" she nodded. "Will you be going before or after pranzo," she asked.

"Probably as soon as I've finished breakfast," I replied. But the thought of my taking a trip on a near-empty stomach, even a trip of only half an hour by car, only challenged her to force-feed me even more.

"*Mangia,*" she said again with the firmness of a mother scolding a reluctant child. "*Mangia.*"

The Cosco Firm

After giving in to Anita and eating more than I planned, including some sausage and peppers that she quickly grilled in the kitchen while I munched on hot rolls, I stood to go.

"Please call Riccardo and tell him I'll need the Maserati back this morning," I said, "*D'accordo?*"

"*Sì, signore,*" Anita nodded, suddenly satisfied with her success over breakfast and with what she thought was the beginning to a new relationship with the capo of the estate.

Driving the old Fiat down the hill toward the winery and turning left before the main building toward the garage, I saw Santo standing there talking to Vito. They watched as I braked in front of Riccardo, already waiting for me at the entrance to his domain. He was wiping his tanned and hairy arms on a rag, but it was not an oily rag that I would have expected to see used by a mechanic. Riccardo was responsible for fixing the cars and machinery of the estate, but he also took care of their looks. He was holding a polishing rag in his hands and had obviously just finished wiping down the shiny surfaces of the Maserati's exterior when I arrived.

Santo knew I was driving the new Maserati but didn't seem to mind. Something in his wry smile convinced me that he expected an American to choose the most expensive machine in the stable. Vito's expression was harder to read. I knew he didn't care about automobiles, and certainly would never dream of spending the money on something like this Maserati. All he cared about were his grapes and his wine. But something about him got my attention. Then I remembered that I wanted to ask him about the vintage, and whether he was pleased with it — or disappointed.

"*Ciao, Santo, Vito,*" I said, waving in their direction and excusing myself from Riccardo for the moment. "How are you?"

"*Ciao, Filippo,*" said Santo as Vito said the same.

"So, Vito, how goes the vintage? Are you pleased?" I asked.

"*Sì,* of course, this is a very good year. We will have a good size crop and, if the rains hold off until we're done picking, the quality will be excellent."

He seemed like his old self, exuberant about the grapes and hopeful for the wine, so I checked my concern for his mood.

"Santo, I'm going to Siena today to talk to Antonio Cosco," I informed him.

"What about? Are you making arrangements for new wines to export?" Santo queried.

"No, no, of course not," I reassured him, noting that Vito was also interested in this development. "I'm following up on your ideas about Nonno Filippo and I just thought that I should talk to his friends and business associates. You know, to see if I can find out any more about his death."

Santo nodded and seemed pleased that I was still on that track; Vito seemed to lose interest when he realized that the conversation no longer dealt with wine.

I walked back over to where Riccardo still stood, and he held out his right hand to me. From it, he dangled the keys to the Maserati, and he offered them to me as if I had just won the rights to this car in a game show.

I drove down the lane and roared out onto the narrow macadam road at the entrance to the family vineyards. There was seldom another vehicle on this road, and I didn't even bother to look anymore as I entered the roadway. The sun was midway toward its zenith, and I was planning to enjoy the curving tree-lined roads between the winery and Siena. In the States, I would have spent these cherished moments of the morning in running shoes or working out at the club, but somehow it felt more appropriate in Italy to enjoy the early morning freshness with a ride in the car.

Besides, I rationalized I had business in town. The investigation had gone poorly so far, and I decided that it was because I had only half-heartedly believed my cousins and not pursued the possible leads with earnestness. I was having too much fun being back in Tuscany, at the Castello dei Trantini, and with Ilsa, and I had already put off looking into the accident too long. This morning, as I sipped the aromatic espresso that Anita served along with the sweet rolls, I reconsidered the available evidence and decided that what the family knew about Nonno Filippo weighed more heavily than the physical evidence of the case. The facts may not be enough to convince Captain Mirelli that a murder had been committed, but my grandfather's penchant for habitual action had nearly convinced me.

I was on my way to the office of the exporter who handled Nonno Filippo's wines. To prove a murder that seemed to have no motive, I decided I would have to get to know all the people associated with the winery, especially those with selfish interests in its activities.

The Maserati rolled up in front of the exporter's offices, a plain-looking, staid building with many layers of repairs to its stucco façade showing through the paint. Other than the few flowering bushes planted haphazardly along the walkway approaching the front door, the building was nondescript, perhaps befitting a building devoted to making profits from another man's labors. As I stepped out of the car, I noticed someone peering out the window at me, half hidden by the heavy drapes hung in front of the glass, and I nodded and smiled at the half-hidden figure within. At my acknowledgment, the eyes turned quickly away, and I walked up to the door.

Before I could even knock, the door was opened by a young woman wearing a colorful, summer dress and staring coolly at me. Prevented from knocking, I was momentarily at a loss, and I just stared at the lovely form in front of me. Her head was tossed slightly to the side, and the long brown hair cascaded down past her shoulders. The bright flower print of the dress enhanced the tanned skin and I watched keenly as she shifted her weight and the neckline rippled to reveal her supple form hidden by the enticingly thin fabric.

"Yes?" she asked finally.

"I am Filippo Trantino. I am the grandson of…"

"Filippo Trantino."

Her cool response was either of disinterest or dislike, and I waited a few seconds to be invited to enter. She guarded the door as if it was her home rather than a place of business, and I hoped she would say something to break the silence.

"I would like to speak to Signor Antonio Cosco. Is he in?"

"Yes," she answered, and finally stepped aside so I could enter.

The office was small, occupied only by two desks and many file cabinets. There were no pictures on the walls, and no other artistic touches to the rather barren atmosphere. It appeared very much like an office that specialized in moving goods from one place to another by contract. Paper was the major concern, and the people who worked here often knew no more about winemaking than the consumer who merely pulled the cork. A frown settled across my face as I contemplated the love showered on the bubbling juice in the winery, to be replaced by the cold, calculated actions of these people concerned only with the money they could make from it.

"How can I help you," I heard from over my shoulder.

A man appeared from a hallway office and extended his hand toward me. He wore the dapper clothes of a man more concerned with appearances than with product. His clean-shaven face and stylishly trimmed hair reminded me of the business majors I had known in college, but he carried with him a distinctly European air that my younger colleagues could only guess at.

"I am Filippo…"

"I know. And I am Antonio Cosco. It is so nice to meet you, Signor Trantino," as his voice switched from a business-like monotone to one with exaggerated kindliness. "I wish we could have met under better circumstances. Would you please come to my office? We will be more comfortable there."

"Thank you," I responded, and we walked down the hallway from which he had come.

His office was as sparsely decorated as the outer room, although here the walls sported an occasional print, usually with wine themes, but some also depicting famous buildings from around Italy. The bookshelves were cluttered with computer printouts and business reports, and the floor to one side of his desk was piled high with bound reports of some sort. I settled into a chair in front of his desk, and he lowered himself slowly into the large, overstuffed chair across from me.

"How can I be of service to you, Signor Trantino?"

"Quite frankly, Signor Cosco, my cousins have discussed with me the possibility that our grandfather's death was not an accident, that someone pushed him out that window."

Cosco was sitting back in his chair, his elbows resting on its upholstered arms, with fingers laced together. His position didn't change, nor did his expression, when I made my bold announcement.

"And so," he responded, "you have come here to find out who might have wanted to kill your grandfather."

"I am interested in learning anything I can about my grandfather's associates, including his business associates, especially during those last few months. If there is any chance that he was murdered, I might be able to uncover the villain by establishing a motive."

"Yes, I remember hearing the polizia say that it was probably not a murder because they could uncover no motive. You do not believe that, Signor Trantino?"

"I admit that so far I have found no motive. But the circumstances of Nonno Filippo's death are indeed suspicious, and I was hoping that you might be able to help me."

"Perhaps you expect to find your motive here, signore?"

I blushed slightly, realizing that he suspected me of suspecting him, but continued.

"I expect only to uncover facts about my grandfather's life that may lead to the murderer. As his broker and exporter, you were a significant part of his financial life. I was hoping that you could help me identify anyone with a possible interest in seeing my grandfather dead."

Cosco sat forward, leaning on his arms stretched wide across the desk, and he peered directly into my eyes. He paused momentarily, as if to take my measure, and spoke with a slow concentration.

"Signor Trantino, you do not know me, and I know that you are still grieving a terrible loss, but you must understand, and believe, that I had no reason whatsoever to kill your grandfather. No one that I know in this establishment had any reason to kill him. True, we made a considerable amount of money from his wines, but this is precisely why we would not have wanted to see anything happen to him. You can check my records," he said, waving his hand at the stacks of papers accumulated on his desk and bookshelves.

"Your grandfather made a lot of money for us. I admired him, and I was grateful that we could retain his contract for so long." Then he smiled and added, "You know, there are many exporters who would love to get the Trantino contract, and many who offered more money, but your grandfather was never interested in making top dollar. The Trantino family signed a contract with my grandfather, Rocco Cosco, fifty-five years ago, and the families have maintained the contract for these many years. Some years the wine was only so-so, and sometimes the exporter was only so-so." He said this with a self-deprecating grin, his left hand outstretched and tipping side to side.

"But we always respected each other, and your grandfather said that was more important than having his face on the cover of *The Wine Press*. He liked our company because he liked our family. I must say the feeling was mutual, from my grandfather to my father to me.

"I didn't know your grandfather that well. It wasn't as if we dined together often, although he was close to my father who was more his age. But when my father died suddenly last year, there was never any doubt that the Trantino contract would be maintained with the same conditions first signed decades ago."

The dark hair and darker eyebrows highlighted his intense face, and the softness of his brown eyes made believing him very easy.

"Thank you, Signor Cosco, for your loyalty, but I didn't mean to imply that I suspected you or an employee of your firm."

"Don't worry, I didn't take it personally," he said, waving away the thought with his right hand. "I just wanted you to know how I felt about the association between your family's vineyards and my family's exporting business." And then, as if it was an afterthought, "Oh, please excuse me for being so rude, would you like something to drink?"

Before I could refuse, he hurried over to the door and, opening it, called out to the young lady in the summer dress.

"Antonina, bring a bottle of the '78 Trantini Riserva. And two glasses."

I couldn't repress a smile, recalling how much I loved the 1978 Castello dei Trantini Chianti Classico Riserva. Vito must have worked magic on that wine; it was truly one of the finest we had ever produced. His instruction to bring two glasses at first struck me as unusual, but I assumed that tasting wines, alone, was a common practice of his and he must have thought it necessary to remind Antonina that this request was for his guest also.

In a few minutes the beautiful young woman returned, brushing by me as the hem of her dress whisked the sweet smell of perfume in my direction. She threw a sideways glance at me without expression as she went about drawing the cork from the wine bottle. She performed this task with such deftness that I was sure she was not a teetotaler, and I watched as she neatly poured two half-glasses of wine, never filling so much that the liquid could not be easily swirled to release its aroma.

She left as quickly as she had arrived, and the door closed quietly behind her. Cosco raised his glass to me and took a tentative sip. He allowed the wine to swirl around in his mouth for a few seconds while he stared blankly at the ceiling. Then, as a slow smile crept across his lips, he swallowed and broke into a pleased grin.

"Yes, I do believe that is the best I have ever tasted from Vito."

I was somewhat unhappy that he would refer to the winemaker rather than the winery, forgetting the many years that the Castello dei Trantini had produced wine before Vito Basiglio was hired.

Then his grin took a mischievous turn, and he added, "Of course, it is not as good as the 1914 or the 1927 made by your great-uncle, Saverio Trantino. Now *there* was a winemaker to remember!"

I smiled wanly at his obvious expertise with wine, especially when it came to the Trantini wines, and I wondered if his knowledge was gained from the business of exporting or whether he had some other interest in the vinous juice itself.

"So, now," he continued, "what can I do for you in this investigation?" He said the last word with a hint of doubt, as if my collection of questions would not amount to a true investigation in his mind.

In fact, his use of the word "investigation" reminded me of how foolish it was for an amateur like me to question what the police had found to be without interest, but Cosco's tone let me know that he was serious, if only for my sake.

"I want to know if there was anyone who might have had a reason to kill my grandfather. Anyone who would have benefited from his death whether that person is in the wine business or not. Even if you suspect someone in my family or, sorry to say, in yours I want to know. The facts surrounding his death are suspicious, but other than that I have no reason to believe he was murdered. So, I must first find a motive."

Cosco thought for a moment, twirling the glass between his thumb and forefinger, and watching as the glycerin in the wine left long streamers down the inside of the glass, the so-called "legs" of wine.

"Your grandfather had only a few dealings in the business world, that much is easy to relate. His contract with the Cosco house was exclusive, although we only handled his exporting. The Trantini wines sold here in Italy were handled by Giovanni della Francia, operating out of Florence. Again, the contract with della Francia was very old, although not as old as that with my family. I believe Filippo Trantino first signed on with della Francia about thirty years ago, but from what I know, there have been no problems since.

"As far as possible culprits at the winery itself, I could not tell you. Perhaps you would know better, since you spend so much time there."

I ignored his comment and continued, "In addition to the Cosco and della Francia families' dealings with Castello dei Trantini, what other business would Filippo Trantino have been involved in?"

"That's just it. There is no other that I can think of. Signor Trantino was a man dedicated to his wine. His associations with the outside world extended only as far as necessary to promote and sell that wine. Although he had many friends, he did not need to work with anyone other than Cosco, della Francia, and those he employed at the winery and vineyards themselves."

"What about his personal business dealings? Did he get involved with anyone who might have wished him dead? I know he didn't gamble or anything like that, but do you know of any excessive debts or commitments made by him? Was there anyone who would have wanted to pressure him, to lean on him, to get something he was un-willing or unable to give?"

"No. You're right he didn't gamble. It wasn't that he was so saintly," and then he laughed, "In fact, I remember hearing stories of the girl-friend he had years ago in town, one he took up with shortly after your grandmother's death." Suddenly realizing his faux pas, he retreated quickly.

"Oh, I didn't mean to suggest anything disreputable. Signor Trantino loved his wife very much, and the stories about he and Sig-nora Grana may not even be true. In any case, they all refer to times after your grandmother was gone."

"Who is this Signora Grana?" I asked.

"Raffaella Grana. A very beautiful woman in her day. Your grandfa-ther supposedly developed an affection for her, and with his dashing appearance and savoir faire, it didn't take long for Signora Grana to lose herself to him. They carried on for quite some time. In fact, many people in town maintain that their love affair lasted right up until his recent death." At this, his brow furrowed, and he looked directly at me.

"You don't think Signora Grana had anything to do with this, do you?"

"I am hardly in a position to make such assumptions, Signor Cosco. This is the first I've even heard her name. I'm surprised that it didn't come up earlier." I shook my head in disbelief, suddenly realizing that Nonno Filippo had a secret liaison that he maintained for a long time, which had completely escaped the knowledge of my cousins and me.

Cosco and I continued discussing possible leads for a little while longer, but my mind was locked onto meeting Raffaella Grana. Unfortunately, this detracted from my listening to what else Cosco had to say, so I terminated the meeting as quickly and comfortably as I could.

"Where could I find Signora Grana?" I asked.

"She lives in Radda. On the east side of the Piazza Vecchia. Ask someone there. I'm sure they'll be able to tell you." And then he added as an afterthought, "You might not want to introduce yourself before you find out where she lives. The mention of the Trantino name in a question about her might raise unwanted suspicions."

"Good idea. Thank you, Signor Cosco. You've been very helpful."

I left through the same room I had first entered and hoped to see Antonina, but she was not there. With Ilsa on my mind, wishing for another chance to look at a beautiful woman made me feel guilty, but I smiled when I admitted to myself that that's what any Italian man would want. Just as I was pulling the door shut behind me, I noticed her standing in the doorway of another office, looking out at me with a curious, unreadable expression on her face.

Il Bar Prato

I settled into the webbed seat at a table in front of the Il Fiaschetteria in Montalcino. The drive from Siena was beautiful, as all the hills and valleys had begun to mix the slightly baked and tawny colors of fall with the vibrant purple and green of the vineyards on either side of the road. The hills yawned up, and then down again, as the Maserati glided over the pavement with perfect confidence.

I had worked up an appetite during my conversation with Cosco, which the wine helped to stimulate, and I was ready for lunch at this little bar before meeting with Sergio Berconi. The waiter brought a pitcher of chilled white wine and a basket of bread, then stood with pad and pencil in hand. I hadn't looked at a menu, didn't even know if they had one, but I assumed that I would just order something simple anyway.

"*Legume grigliate,*" I began, "*e pollo con limone e carciofe.*"

"*Si, signore,*" he replied, but he still didn't move. He was a young man with a thick mop of hair on his head and a day's growth of beard on his chin. He was neither pleasant nor gruff, just ready to take the order and return to the kitchen; but he obviously had decided that grilled vegetables and chicken with lemon and artichokes wasn't enough food.

"Okay," I nodded in English, "*anche, zuppe di pesce ed insalata mista.*" Once I had added a soup and salad, the waiter then seemed content I was ordering enough to make up a whole meal and, quickly jotting all this down, walked away.

I had come to realize that Italians had certain ideas about food and what constitutes a proper meal. In one restaurant I frequented in Rome, Ristorante Regina, the woman who owned the place and ran the kitchen took a maternal interest in my welfare. Whenever she thought I wasn't ordering enough food to maintain my good health, she would simply add dishes to my order without asking. Of course, I paid for the additional food; but she wasn't trying to make more money, she just couldn't understand why anyone would order less than the right amount. In this way, the waiter at Il Fiaschetteria was adjusting my order to ensure that I got the proper nourishment. It's true, not all restaurants pressured the customers this way, but most probably wondered at Americans who would sit down to nothing but a salad and basket of bread.

While waiting for my meal to arrive, I called home to bring my parents up to date on the events and the investigation into Nonno Filippo's death. "No," I told them, "there's nothing new. Everyone agrees that no one would want to kill him. Yes," I assured them, "I've thought about my responsibilities," and hoped they realized that I meant both in Tuscany and in America.

"Are you meeting new people there?" my mother asked. I couldn't help but think she meant Ilsa, but how my mother would have heard about this new woman in my life, I couldn't tell.

"Yes, many new people, including some of Nonno's business associates." I hoped that would divert her to less risky conversation.

"Don't trust everything they say. And if you get down to the winery shop, ship some of the olive oil to me. And say hello to that pretty girl who works there."

Okay, that's as close as I wanted to get to maternal manipulation and, putting aside doubts as to her source of information, I closed the call saying that my food had arrived and I was going to have to ring off.

The chilled wine was good, even though it was white wine in this haven of red wine. I didn't even ask for it; sometimes wine just seemed to arrive at restaurant tables in Tuscany, like water.

The food was even better. The mixed salad was made with the freshest of ingredients; the lettuce tasted as though it had just been picked, still even a bit warm from the sun. Soup would ordinarily be an odd choice for midday in summer, but fish soup in Italy is usually served less than piping hot, the better to show off the diverse flavors of the mussels, clams, and shrimp swimming in a broth of herbs and translucent onions. The grilled vegetables were superb, the criss-crossing of grill marks lending a slightly charred flavor to the summer sweetness of the red peppers, zucchini, and tomatoes on the plate. The chicken was beautiful to look at and fantastic to taste. The cutlet had been pounded nearly flat then tossed quickly into the skillet along with the quartered artichoke hearts and lemon wedges. All this was sautéed in a hot skillet, then doused with white wine and a few squeezes of lemon juice from the remaining half of the fruit, and delivered steaming hot to my table.

I lingered over the meal a bit longer than I would normally when dining alone. I wanted to savor the food, but also to take in the scenery around me. The restaurant sat on one side of a narrow piazza in the center of Montalcino. Next door was another bar, and standing tall in the center of the commons was one of the bell towers that had survived the centuries intact. The sun had moved overhead but I was shielded from its direct rays by the umbrella over my table.

The people who populated the piazza at this hour were a social bunch, more talkative perhaps because it was mealtime and they expected to eat well then rest for a couple of hours before returning to their places of work. Siesta in Italy was a time-honored tradition, one that harkened back to the more agricultural era of the country, when nearly all of the population worked outside during the day and needed a break from the sun. They would retire from their labors, eat a satisfying meal, then fall asleep and wait for the hottest temperatures to recede.

These days, most working Italians find jobs inside, but air conditioning is still not common, so the middle of the day can be quite stifling. I'm convinced that this is just an excuse, however; I think Italian men and women long for that break in the middle of their day to lay their heads back and rest. Most do not sleep, as Americans imagine, they just stop working, and instead spend a little bit of their day with family and friends. It's a very social time, as evidenced by the increased excitement and conversation in the piazza before me.

Americans have a hard time understanding this routine. Most of my friends back in the States say they couldn't imagine stopping for a few hours, especially with lots of food and wine, then restarting again at about three o'clock. And they say they wouldn't want to work until seven or eight o'clock every evening to make room for that midday break. But the Italians are just as confused when they hear of Americans working from early morning into the evening with no more than a quick sandwich and a short break in the middle. They can't understand how Americans can toil uninterruptedly for so many hours. Italians make the point that their *cena*, their important evening meal, doesn't usually begin until eight or nine o'clock, so they're not missing anything by coming home later.

I shook my head and smiled to myself as I considered these opposing views and knew that each one would stubbornly cling to the routine he was used to. But for me, at that moment, I was certainly enjoying the Italian schedule.

When the meal concluded, I poured another glass of wine from the pitcher dripping with perspiration in the heat. In a few moments, the waiter brought my check and I noticed the billing information at the bottom: *vino per uno.* I had come across this before in Italy where wine is often served in some bulk form, such as this label-less pitcher. I was charged a single price, a small fee, for whatever wine I had consumed — "wine for one." If there had been someone else at the table, it would simply have been *vino per due.*

A walk was in order, *una passeggiata,* a routine Italians liked as a way of aiding digestion and working off their meals. Americans always marvel at how Italians can remain relatively slim with these gargantuan meals they enjoy. Walking is the key. Instead of moving from the dinner table to the couch, as Americans are wont to do, Italians get up after a meal and move around, sometimes walking arm-in-arm through the piazze and streets of their community, before they settle down for a rest.

So, with this in mind, I decided that a walk would do me good. I still had a bit of time before my meeting with Sergio Berconi and I wanted to walk off my lunch.

Montalcino, renowned for its wine, should also get credit for its many small shops selling ceramics. My mother's vast collection of bowls, plates, and pitchers from this country came mostly from this little town. As I walked, I visited some of the shops in search of something, anything, to bring back to my villa. I found a large platter that I thought would look good perched above the door leading into the villa from the loggia. I considered the price, then considered whether the colors were right. As the man behind the table offered suggestions, certain that this would be perfect for whatever I decided, he also had to manage a slightly unruly preschool-aged child dangling from his leg.

I passed up the sale, visited a few more shops, then walked slowly in the direction of the Piazza Cavour, a little square in the center of town with three large and withered trees shading a parched, grassless patch of land dotted with dilapidated wooden benches at the perimeter. The Piazza Cavour was in the main part of town, but its state of disrepair revealed the extent to which Montalcino had aged. Once a thriving republic and the envy of surrounding cities, Montalcino had retained some of its original grace, and the *Fortezza* and wine bars were still major tourist attractions, but the city was now described as charming, not vibrant.

On one side of the piazza was Il Bar Prato, a tiny place whose tables spilled out onto the roadway in front. There were only a couple of tables inside, squeezed close to the counter from which wine, beer, coffee, and snacks were served. There was a sidewalk just outside the door, but the cars that careened around the building from the side street usually cut the corners off the turn so sitting even a few feet beyond the door of Il Bar Prato was risky.

I slipped through the afternoon crowd and ordered *un caffé*, that Italians naturally understood to be an espresso. To get a cup of brewed coffee the way Americans liked it, a customer would have to order *un caffé Americano.*

The waiter looked at me, eyebrows raised, with an espresso cup in one hand and a slender glass bottle with a long neck in his other hand. "*Corretto?*" he asked over the din.

"No," I replied, I didn't want my coffee "corrected" with a shot of grappa. Throughout Europe, alcohol is more a part of daily intake than in America. The Italians and French, especially, don't share Americans fear that regular consumption of wine and spirits will somehow incapacitate them. So, they have made it part of the cultural landscape. In this case, the waiter was simply asking the logical question, would I want my coffee corrected with a bit of grappa. He wasn't put off when I said no; he just thought he should ask.

I took my "uncorrected" coffee to an outside table set against the wall, leaving sufficient room between my chair and the tire-marked corner to avoid danger. I expected Sergio to arrive at any time, though I wasn't sure how I'd recognize him. He and Nonno Filippo had been friends for years, but since I didn't normally socialize with septuagenarians, his visits to the Castello usually took place when I was not here. I knew I'd met him before and thought I might be able to pick him out of a crowd but decided to stay alert just the same.

In a moment, a courtly gentleman in a starched white shirt, neatly pressed trousers, and brown fedora approached the bar. He was about the right age, and his prim appearance and stately grace reminded me of Nonno Filippo. "Birds of a feather," I thought, and decided this must be Signor Sergio Berconi.

Standing, I offered my hand, and said, "*Buon giorno. Sono* Filippo Trantino."

"*Sì,*" he responded with a wide smile and a firm handshake. "*Sì,* Filippo, you look just like your grandfather."

"I take that as a compliment," was my response, and his easy affability put me at ease.

Sergio was about the same age as my grandfather, with the tanned face and ruddy skin of a man who has worked outside most of his life. His hands were broad and strong, and he sat stiffly erect in the chair next to me as if he had spent a lifetime mindful of his posture. I recalled that he was not rich, nor particularly well educated. He owned an ironworks shop and worked hard, and he was proud of the business he had built up over the years. Without any notice, a reedy young man from Il Bar Prato delivered a tumbler to Sergio with a reddish liquid and the scent of Campari, setting the icy glass down in front of the older man without speaking. I guessed my friend was a regular at the bar.

Sergio took a thankful sip from the glass, sighed in pleasure, then let his smile slip momentarily while he told me how saddened he was by the news of Nonno Filippo's death.

"A terrible thing," he said, shaking his bowed head. "For a man to fall from the heights. How could such a thing happen to Filippo?"

It was obviously a rhetorical question, but I decided to take hold of it for my own reasons.

"It's true, a terrible thing. Did you know, Signor Berconi, that some people don't consider his death an accident?"

This brought a quick reaction from Sergio, but he didn't speak immediately. He seemed like he wanted to consider the comment, as if he wanted to look at the recent events from a new angle.

"No, I didn't know that, and I don't believe it," he said finally. "If it wasn't an accident, then it would have been murder. No one would have wanted to murder Filippo. I know everything about him, and every friend he had, and no one would have done such a thing."

"It's not the friends I'm thinking about," I replied, shrugging off the comment as if it was too obvious to make. "Did he have any enemies?"

"Do you mean all the other wineries who wished they could sell as much wine as he did?" he asked with a laugh. "No, not enemies, as you would say, but Filippo might have left some competitors wishing he wasn't around anymore. I don't think any of them would have done this. Besides, he was in the Castello, no? When it happened?

Who could have been there without Anita, or Vito, or one of the other employees knowing about it?"

I turned the conversation in other directions, discussing Antonio Cosco and Giovanni della Francia, business associates that might have had a less-than-personal perspective on Nonno Filippo's life and activities. Sergio shook his head with the mention of each name, explaining at length why these people not only liked my grandfather, but made money from his success, so they wouldn't want to lose him. I raised other names, with minor connections to the Castello dei Trantini, and got the same response from Sergio, taking sips at intervals from his glass of Campari.

"What about Raffaella?" I asked, switching suddenly to a totally different tact.

He eyed me carefully, took a sip of his drink, then said, "*chi?*"

He might have been a great friend to my grandfather, but he was a poor actor, and my look and muttered "huff" made him realize that I wasn't buying his feigned ignorance.

"Raffaella Grana," I said, "I believe she and my grandfather had a relationship." Just a little emphasis on the last word.

"Oh, yes," Sergio said, waving the thought away, as if relationships of this nature were part of the fabric of Italian life, but still not something talked about.

"What about her?" I pressed.

Sergio didn't want to talk about this part of Nonno Filippo's life, so he stalled. Looking at me again, he saw that I wouldn't be too patient, and since I was considering the possibility of foul play in the "accident," I would want to have all the information I could get.

He took his time, sipping now from the second tumbler of Campari delivered by the waiter, and told me about Signora Grana and Nonno Filippo. Yes, they had a relationship. No, not while my grandmother was alive. No, he didn't think it was a physical relationship, anyway. Sergio said "physical" with some reluctance, since he wasn't comfortable talking about that with me.

Sergio was withholding details he thought were irrelevant, and I continued to press for more answers until I, too, became uncomfortable. I came to realize that my curiosity about Nonno Filippo's secret life was overlapping with my interest in solving the mystery of his death, and I decided that I should tackle one thing at a time.

Slowly, our conversation moved to more convivial subjects as I realized that Sergio's interest in focusing on the death was ebbing. We talked about Nonno Filippo, how he lived and what he liked most in life. Sergio's memories were more complete than mine, and reflected experiences shared by a contemporary of my grandfather, but the recollections were consistent. I knew the patriarch of the Trantino clan was a lively, amorous, and hard-working man, someone loved and trusted by all. He was intense about his business and his life, and this intensity produced better wine, better profits, and more thrilling life experiences in general. It should have come as no surprise to me that he would have been attracted to a woman described as a true beauty — just as he had been attracted to my grandmother when she was young.

We sipped our drinks, mine had by then switched from coffee to anisette, and talked for another hour about life at the Castello dei Trantini.

"What will you do, Filippo?" Sergio asked. It was a direct question and, although he was a relative stranger to me, I didn't mind the obviously personal tone. He and my grandfather had been friends since before I was born and Sergio might well have known more about the Castello, its wines, and its history, than I did. His question hinted at his concern for the future of the Castello dei Trantini.

"I'm not sure yet, but I'm thinking of staying on."

Sergio nodded and smiled, as if this would be a good thing. Then, with a twinkle in his eye, he reminded me that there might be some "good Italian woman" to help me make my decision. As he did this, my thoughts drifted to Ilsa. I smiled, sipped the last of my anisette, and we said goodbye.

The House of Della Francia

A few days later, I decided to pay a visit to the house of Giovanni della Francia. I knew the younger della Francia, having met him at various social functions that were popular among the wine merchants. He, Paolo, was the eldest son of the founder, Giovanni, and carried on the business for his aging and ailing father. Paolo had aspirations that were more in tune with the greedy wholesalers of Bordeaux and was always devising schemes to increase the yield of the vineyards, a subject he knew little about except that it translated into more profits for himself.

"There is only so much quality in each acre of land," Nonno Filippo would say. "If we force the land to share its quality with too many grapes, its character is spread too thin and the entire crop suffers because of it." But Paolo wasn't interested in this. He assumed that the reputation of the winery would sell the product, even if in the years to come the quality slowly ebbed and the reputation was lost.

He was often seen at social events cornering one of the estate owners and, in hushed tones, describing how the world had finally awakened to the wonders of wine and that we must find new ways to pry greater yields from the acres we managed in order to satisfy the craving. He was right about the world's newfound desire for wine; but it was precisely now that the great winemakers of Tuscany, Piedmont, and Bordeaux should focus their efforts, strengthen their reputations, and convince the new and old customers that their product was preferable to other beverages. A reduction in the overall quality of the wine was the opposite of what they wanted.

Giovanni della Francia would have had nothing to do with such tactics. He had grown up in Tuscany and loved the wines from his region even before he had a financial relationship with the winemakers. Later, when he opened his business to buy and sell the Tuscan wines, he remained true to his first love and always dealt fairly with the producers. Giovanni felt that his business survived only in the reflected brilliance of the wine trade, and he secretly thanked the vignerons and winemakers for allowing their art to fatten his purse.

It's a shame his son learned only Giovanni's knack for business and not his respect for the merchandise. Paolo was very good at managing the house of Giovanni della Francia, so good that his father slowly delegated more and more of the tasks to him over the years, admitting sometimes openly that Paolo had become better at the duties than he himself had been.

But whenever he would make such an admission, a frown would pass briefly across Giovanni's face, an outward sign that he never forgot his son's preference for profit over quality, for expedience over perfection. It was this lurking frown that prevented Giovanni from acquitting himself of the last of the duties of the house of della Francia, the yearly contractual agreements with the winemakers, until his health turned irreparably for the worse. Then, Giovanni realized that he would not long be able to continue with the demands of the business, and he reluctantly agreed to delegate that last of responsibilities to his penurious son.

As the long, dusty road opened up into one of the highways leading to Florence, I geared down and tuned the radio to one of the stations in the area. The melodic Italian songs crooned at me from the dashboard as I watched the familiar scene come into view.

Here was my favorite city in the world: Florence. The green hills and vineyards that surrounded it slowly closed in on the red-roofed buildings and the blue waters of the Arno River as it wound lazily through the clusters of houses on the outskirts of the city. I steered the Maserati down the Lungarno that stretched along the banks of the river and passed quickly through the crowded intersection at the base of the Ponte Vecchio, the home of some of Italy's most renowned gold merchants. A few blocks past the bustling crowd of tourists and shoppers, I made a quick left turn toward the center of the city and past the magnificent churches that crowded this section of Florence. A little farther down the road I drove by San Marco, the monastery that housed saints and sinners, popes and heretics, depending on what era each was born into.

I glanced at the paper in my hand to check the address of the house of della Francia and came to an abrupt halt just before nearly missing it. I checked once more to verify that I was at the correct house, and then climbed out of the car.

Paolo was in his office, bent hard over a desk full of papers, as I entered the room. He looked up quickly as I entered, somewhat disconnected at first from the present, then recognized me and with a broad smile invited me to sit down. His expansive gestures convinced me that he thought I would be the person to deal with concerning the Trantini wines, so I decided to go along with this for a moment to distract him from any thought as to the true nature of my visit.

"So, Signor Trantino, it's been so long since I've seen you. How have you been? I was just thinking the other day that I should visit the Castello to pay my respects."

His almost jovial attitude was wholly inappropriate for what condolences he was attempting to pass on, so I decided to accept it as his inadequate response to the situation, but otherwise I ignored it.

"I'm so sorry about your grandfather. I trust this unfortunate accident will have no effect on the continued goodwill between our families."

His slobbering exaggerations and pandering made me nauseous, but I allowed him to continue, hoping that soon he would be out of wind.

"As you know, we have always held your family in the highest esteem, and the wines produced at the Castello are among the finest in

Tuscany. It was a great tragedy," he said, looking dutifully downward. "But now what can I do for you?"

"Actually," I began, deciding to take the swift, brusque approach with this rodent, "I am investigating the possibility that my grandfather was murdered."

I waited for my words to take effect. I was interested in seeing whether such an abrupt statement would cause a shift in his attitude, a glimmer of conscience if he had any.

"Well," Paolo responded slowly, "that *is* a stunning undertaking! And what leads you to believe that Signor Trantino's death was anything but what the polizia have said, that is, an accident?"

"Certain things, but I am not at liberty to divulge them at this time. Do you know why someone might want to kill my grandfather? Have you heard of anything that might have happened in the recent past that would lead you to believe that someone would want him dead?"

"Yes," he answered too quickly, "I've always wondered about that Antonio Cosco."

"His exporter?" I replied, somewhat in disbelief at his accusing tone.

"Yes. He has always seemed too anxious to get more of Signor Trantino's wines. As if none should be sold here in this country."

In trying to prey on the self-interested motives of others, his own self-interest showed clearly.

"What would that have to do with my grandfather's murder?"

"Signor Filippo," he began, and his retreat to the familiar address annoyed me, "please do not assume that your grandfather was murdered, as your words indicate you do. Surely, it could have happened, but I know of no one at this time who shares your beliefs."

"There are others, Signor Paolo," I said, stressing his first name and studying the effect of turning the casual tables on him. "What I need is your cooperation, not cross-examination. Can you help me in identifying anyone with a possible motive?"

"No, quite frankly, I cannot. But if I hear of anything that might be of interest, I'll let you know."

His dismissal of me, and the subject, irritated me. I stood up, shook his hand, and departed.

I drove back along the roads I had known since my childhood. As I pressed harder on the accelerator, I felt the Maserati leap ahead as the clouds of dust billowed out from behind, cleansing me of the feeling I had about Paolo della Francia. I could see a train rolling along its ancient tracks in the distance, and on the hills to the east, pickers working along the rows of vines. This was the land that I loved, here, I felt at home. Here, life's dreams seem to come real, and the sky and earth combined with the spirit in one continuous spiral of life. I could feel the scales balancing my choice between America and Italy were tipping.

Raffaella

My next visit was to see Raffaella Grana in Radda. As Cosco suggested, I avoided the customary self-introduction when inquiring as to the Grana residence and was rewarded with helpful information.

The piazza was as busy as others I had encountered in Italy, even though it was a relatively small town. But the main piazza of every town was usually the center of activity for the community. Often, there would be a finely sculpted fountain recalling the glory days of Medieval Europe, and cobblestone or large quarry-stone steps leading up to it. It was about midday when I arrived, and there were crowds at almost every doorstep, people chattering about the events of the day or the prospects of the local soccer team in the upcoming championship.

Three men were sitting at a table outside Il Bar Sportivo, playing chess and sipping a dark liquid from tall, handled glasses. I caught the scent of some sort of coffee liqueur, and I welcomed the aromas. When asked about Signora Grana, they both pointed to a balcony across the piazza and my eyes followed their indication.

I could see where she lived, on the east side of the Piazza Vecchia, with a fine view of the church called Chiesa di Santa Cristina. The balcony had a railing featuring delicate designs of iron filigree and two large flowerpots overflowing with bougainvillea. The gossamer lace curtains that hung in the open doorway billowed inward toward the apartment as the gentle breeze wafted across the courtyard.

Like most of the residential buildings in Italy, the exterior of this one wore an undistinguished face. Most of the houses and apartments I had seen in Italy were the same: plain to the point of being drab on the outside but beautifully styled on the inside. Where American homes have linoleum floors, even poor Italians have marble. Where Americans have concrete, the Italians have stone. Where Americans have generic furniture, Italians have beautifully carved, inlaid wood tables covered with lace, sideboards festooned with beautiful vases filled with fresh flowers, and delicate sheer curtains that dance as a gentle breeze blows through the windows.

I ascended the stairs and knocked on the door to the second-floor apartment. In a moment the door opened and, as if she recognized me immediately, Signora Grana swung it wide to admit me, a beaming smile marred only a bit by the tears that started to glisten in her eyes.

"Signor Filippo, it's so good to see you."

I had never met her before, but it was obvious that she knew me by sight. As I walked through the foyer into her living room, I saw a number of photographs of Nonno Filippo and other members of my family, even one of my grandfather and grandmother together in the garden in the back of the house. She greeted me warmly, as if I was a member of her family, and begged me to sit while she went to get something for us to drink.

While Raffaella was occupied in the kitchen, I looked around the room at all the memorabilia from the Trantino family and another group of people I took to be her family. There were no photographs that included members of both families, but all other indications — save for the one picture of my grandmother and grandfather together — would have led a stranger to conclude that Raffaella Grana was married to Nonno Filippo.

There were photographs of many of my cousins, I among them, and other delicate mementoes of times past. Taking in all the things around me I recalled Sergio Berconi's reluctance to talk about this and quickly dismissed the notion that Signora Grana and Nonno Filippo had known each other only since my grandmother's death some ten years earlier. I shook my head in disbelief, and felt a wave of resentment welling up inside of me, but calmed it and tried to wait until I had learned more about what took place between these two people. The restful atmosphere of the room put me at ease, and the photographs of so many familiar faces almost made me feel as if I belonged there.

Signora Grana returned and set a tray down on the low table between the two couches. She sat next to me and poured Campari over the ice in the two short glasses there.

I looked closely at her while her eyes were diverted with the task of pouring. She was not as old as my grandfather, but much older than me. She was quite beautiful, as everyone had said. Her gray-flecked, auburn hair was tied back from her neck and the straight line of her chin gave her a noble appearance. She had delicate hands, as if she had never done hard labor, and her slight figure completed a picture of a woman who was well-groomed, well-educated, and still yearning to live and love.

"I am so happy to meet you," she said, raising her glass in salute. "I had often hoped to meet you before this time, but unfortunately it could not be."

"I'm happy to meet you also, Signora Grana." I decided to avoid saying that I had never heard her name until yesterday. "I feel we have both lost someone very dear to us."

"Yes," she said, and her eyes grew moist again. "I loved Filippo very much. Yes, I know he was afraid to introduce me to the family, but it was only because of what happened before."

Puzzled, I asked her what she meant. Her dark eyes had an intensity to them, and she paused for a moment before answering.

"Filippo and I first met and fell in love twenty-seven years ago."

She paused again, giving me time to reflect. But twenty-seven years! My eyes narrowed as I tried to maintain my objectivity.

"You see," she continued, "we have loved each other for a long time, but we have never been lovers." With a gentle laugh she added, "Your grandfather's classical attitudes would never have permitted him to have an affair, and I have to admit that an affair is not what I wanted.

So, we continued as if we were only good friends, meeting here whenever we could, loving each other with our words and our eyes. Your grandmother was a very lucky woman, Filippo."

"And very deserving," I added, somehow feeling the need to defend my grandmother. Then I softened. "I'm sorry. I didn't mean that the way it sounded. But if you felt that way all this time, why didn't you and Nonno Filippo get married after my grandmother died?"

"By that time, enough had been said about our relationship." There was a wistful look to her as she recalled the years that had slipped away, but she continued. "Although nothing ever happened between us, it would have been impossible to protect your grandfather's reputation if he married his 'whore.' " She said this with a real sadness in her eyes, and I knew the label was unfairly applied by her to stress a point.

"I refused him, actually," she continued, straightening up and regaining her composure. "I said that it would demean the memory of his dear wife to take another woman so late in life. He was not as young as me, you know," she said with a mischievous wink.

I knew. If they had known each other for twenty-seven years, Signora Grana would have been a relatively young woman when my grandfather was then in his forties.

"He was a handsome man, though. All his life. I have pictures of him here from when he was a young man and a captain in the Italian air force. Look at this one," she said, swooping one photograph off the end table near her. "Isn't he impressive? I even have pictures of the rest of his family, and you too, Filippo. Look here."

She displayed a picture of me standing between rows of vines with Nonno Filippo. I recognized it immediately. It was my grandfather's favorite photograph of me. We were standing in the di Rosa vineyard. Everyone always said he liked that picture because it showed the best products of good soil and good family.

Raffaella seemed to be enjoying this reminiscing, all the more since she was able to do so with a member of the Trantino family, and I was pleased at her obvious joy. Her voice was light and lively as she talked about me, Nonno Filippo, and my cousins, and her eyes sparkled as she recounted some of the stories from the past that she knew only through my grandfather's telling. As I listened to her, she became more a part of my family and I realized how easy it would have been for her to fit into the Trantino clan. But after some time, I felt the need to change the subject.

"Signora Grana," I began, "Santo, Rita, and I believe that Nonno Filippo's death might not have been an accident."

The glow of the past twenty minutes disappeared from her face, and her eyes misted over. The change seemed not so much from my startling news as from the realization that it was commonly accepted. I decided to press this opening.

"Do you think that this could be true? Do you have any reason to think that someone would have wanted to kill Nonno Filippo?"

For a few moments she was silent, just staring intently at me. Then lowering her head, she spoke.

"Yes, I think that is possible, but many things are possible."

"I'm not speaking in the purely pedantic sense, Signora Grana. I am asking whether you think there was a reason someone would have wanted him killed."

"There are many things we don't understand, Filippo. And accidents do happen, even when we think they cannot, or should not. Yes, it's possible it was not an accident," she said, getting up and walking across the room, "but sometimes accidents are made out of intentions. Sometimes a person means for one thing to happen and something else happens. We cannot always be in control of these things."

She seemed to be talking in riddles, but I could tell that there was truth hidden behind the layers of her speech.

"Signora Grana, I am serious about this. If you have some information that may help us identify the murderer of my grandfather, you must tell me. Surely, you would want the person to be apprehended."

"No, Filippo, not 'surely.' Perhaps your grandfather would not want this person to be identified. Perhaps these tragic events must be left alone, and let the present bury the past."

Her words intrigued me, as if she knew not only what might have transpired, but what in fact actually occurred. It even seemed somehow that her pleas about accidents not always seeming so to be a sort of admission.

"Signora Grana, I do not wish to cause you any more pain than you have already experienced, but it does seem from your words that you know things that might help me." Then, swallowing hard and searching for the right words, "Did you see Nonno Filippo the day he died?"

"Yes, earlier in the day." She looked away toward the large bouquet of brightly colored flowers in the vase on the sideboard. "He was very agitated then, as if something was terribly wrong."

"Did he tell you what was bothering him?"

"A little, but he would not wish you to know."

"Me? Why wouldn't he want me to know?"

"It was something that happened in the past. He had only just discovered it. But he considered it the greatest secret and wouldn't even tell me very much about it."

"What did he say?"

She hesitated.

"Only that the Castello was in jeopardy. That something had happened a long time before and that the news of it threatened the Castello in some way. He wouldn't explain any further, except I could see he was very worried. He loved the estate so much, Filippo."

"Yes, we all do. There is nothing else, Signora Grana?"

"No. That was all." She looked at me with large, tearful eyes, and I tried to comfort her, but realized that my mind was on the Castello and hers was on losing the man in her life.

It was difficult to resume our earlier, lighter conversation, so only a little more was said before I excused myself.

"I'm sorry, but I have many things to do. I will stop by again if it is alright."

"Oh, yes, please do, Filippo. I would so welcome you."

When I left, I noticed that the old men standing in the piazza were paying more attention to me, and I saw one of them pointing in the direction of Signora Grana's apartment.

Piecing It Together

While driving back to the Castello, I was confident now that I could deal less emotionally with my grandfather's death and was beginning to relax and contemplate a permanent return to Tuscany. My mind wandered back to recent events, including my time with Ilsa, and how completely I was being absorbed into the culture my parents left behind twenty years before.

I had unconsciously abandoned many of my American habits, habits that I clung to before for my re-entry into life across the ocean, but now I felt that letting them go was safe. And in letting my American traditions slough off, I felt like my Italian self was emerging. It was an alter ego that I thought was long lost, but it resurfaced with ease and made the thoughts of remaining in Tuscany easier to contemplate.

With lots of time to think during the ride back from Radda, I also considered Nonno Filippo's last night in the wine library. I pieced together a reasonable chronology of his actions, knowing what I did about his nearly unchanging routine. I imagined everything that he did, or must have done, and I could picture the scene so clearly that I almost believed I could identify the murderer simply by closing my eyes and seeing him.

I recalled how Nonno Filippo would put his right index finger on the top of each bottle of wine as he studied the label, peering down at it and considering its potential before sampling. He would then begin on the left, working his way across the array of bottles one at a time.

He would pour a generous measure into the glass and walk toward the already-open window with a contented look on his face. His visage always seemed to be a mixture of seriousness and pleasure as he no doubt reminded himself that this was work, but knowing that so many other people would laugh at the use of this word — "work" — to describe what he was doing.

Looking out the window with a sip of each wine, he would be very satisfied with his life. "We are lucky creatures," he reminded me often, raising a glass for emphasis. "We have been given this wonderful estate and the wine it yields. We should appreciate it." And during these daily rituals of tasting, he no doubt reveled in the full meaning of that toast.

As the picture gained clarity in my mind, I unconsciously pressed harder on the accelerator pedal and the Maserati sped faster as I neared the Castello. I was so sure of the scene my mind conjured up for me that I wanted to test it out in the wine library before the image faded.

When I arrived, Vito was walking around the corner of the winery with an elderly woman that I first thought must be his wife. Then I remembered that he had never married, and that this must be the sister I'd met years ago. They saw me get out of the car, and Vito led Elena in my direction as if to introduce us.

"Signor Filippo, this is my sister, Elena Maria Verelli. I believe you have met before."

"Yes," Elena answered for me, "we have met. *Buon giorno*, Signor Filippo. I remember you from the time you were born, here in the Castello." Her words showed familiarity, but her tone was distant. I remembered her with fondness but wondered whether my years away had changed our relationship.

Many memories came back to me, the early years of my life spent living like a young prince in his castle. Yes, I remembered Elena clearly now. I remembered that she would play with me when I was a child, much like a grandmother would with her children's children. By that time, she was married to Carlo Verelli, and their two children had already given them grandchildren, and yet she still played kindly with me.

"It's very nice to see you again, Signora. Will you be here long enough to have dinner with us tonight?"

"No," Vito answered for her. "She must return this evening to her family. But thank you, Signor Filippo."

I turned from Vito and Elena and walked up the stairs to the Castello. Without bothering to stop, I went directly to the wine library, threw open the doors and walked across the room to the window. I threw the window open so quickly that the shutters banged as the metal latches fell back against the stone of the outside walls.

I heard a gasp uttered from below and, looking out, saw that my impetuous action had caught Vito and Elena unaware. The sudden sound coming from the window they knew Nonno Filippo had fallen out of produced an unfortunate effect on them, and I leaned out and apologized for startling them.

Turning around, I surveyed the room, then strode back across the carpet to the door through which I had entered. Then I assumed my position, throwing back my shoulders and puffing out my chest to act the part of Nonno Filippo as best I could, and I looked back at the room. I soon realized that there were no wine bottles or glasses on the massive table in the center of the room. It was not four o'clock yet, the time when Beppo would be delivering the wines for me to taste, and the stark emptiness of the shining surface brought a frown to my face. With shoulders slumping and chest caved in, I rushed out of the room and down to the cellar where I gathered a careless few bottles and tucked them under my arm.

Going past the worktable near the wine racks, I scooped up a handful of the glasses designated for tasting, those with the well-rounded bowls and crystal-clear glass. Then I rushed back up to the wine library and set the bottles and glasses on the table. I opened all the bottles, careful to leave the cork perched at the top of each, and resumed my position at the door to the room. Once again imitating Nonno Filippo's robust, barrel-chested posture, I looked long and hard at the scene around me.

Marching slowly into the room, with my eyes ever on the bottles of wine before me, I stopped just short of the table as I had seen my grandfather do. I clasped my hands behind me, leaned forward to read the labels of all the bottles of wine on the table, and nodded in anticipation. Then, pouring samples from the bottles, I lifted the glasses one at a time, slowly, to examine the contents.

At this point, the ritual became less like mimicry and more like sheer pleasure. I felt a little guilty knowing that when — if — Beppo discovered what I was doing he would feel that he'd been upstaged, so I stole a quick look at my watch. Still time. I continued with the exercise.

With my family's long focus on wine and my regular trips back to the Castello, it was "in my blood" as my American friends like to jest. But it's true that I always welcomed an opportunity to taste new wines, even when the moment is filled with melodrama, as it was that day. But despite my interest in discovering some small segment of the mystery through this process, I would not let it detract from my enjoyment of the wines themselves.

They were all red, and all slightly dry in the tradition of the noble red wines of Italy. The first bottle yielded a tart, acidic wine, not yet ready for the market but one that showed promise for future drinking. I made a mental note of the label and decided to try it again in about three years.

The second wine was not as dry, offering some complexity and depth, with a hint of blackberries on the nose, finishing with a long, well-rounded taste of aged Nebbiolo grapes. Looking again at the bottle, I saw that I was right. It was from Piedmont, where Nebbiolo reigns supreme.

I proceeded to taste until each wine had had its moment. One reminded me of a woman I once knew. I was sure we'd had a bottle of that wine one night at the club near my home. I look at the label; it was a French Syrah. "Ah," I said smiling to the empty room; that *was* what we had that night. And I laughed when I remembered I had promised Cheryl that if I ever tasted that wine again, I would think of her. I kept my promise.

I returned to the second bottle and poured myself a half glass of it. Then, staring at the open window, I was brought sharply back to my reason for beginning this drama. I raised the glass in my right hand, cradling the stem gently between thumb and forefinger, and walked toward the window. I faced out, looking at the di Rosa vineyards, and soon found myself lost in thought. First, I imagined my childhood and could almost see myself running and laughing between the vines. I saw Nonno Filippo, too old to run around with me, but standing there grandly, with his hands on his hips, watching as his favorite grandson played among those plants that had meant his life.

I blinked to chase the emerging tears from my eyes. When I looked again, I saw my parents standing in front of the taxi, waving good-bye to Nonno Filippo, as we departed on our journey to America many years ago. I wondered how he felt that first time afterwards standing at this window looking into the vineyards he wouldn't see us in again for such a long time.

The tears now ran again and, coming back to myself, I tried to control them and get on with the business at hand. I looked at the vineyards below, thinking to myself that this was the last thing my grandfather saw.

Then I stopped. No. It wasn't the last thing he saw. He fell out the window backwards, so he was facing the room. What did he see there?

I turned and faced the table, with my back to the open window. With the glass still perched between my thumb and forefinger, I carefully scanned the room. Seeing no footprints on the carpet, I tried to imagine the person who would track in the mud. If there had been prints when Nonno Filippo entered, he would have noticed it and probably complained right away. Someone would know about the complaint, but no one had mentioned it so far. (I made a mental note to start asking about that.) That meant that there was probably no mud on the carpet when he first entered the room. Therefore, whoever tracked it in followed Nonno Filippo into the wine library.

I noticed that I was leaning back and my hands were now resting on the windowsill, the wine glass still in my right hand. Nonno Filippo must have been turned around by something or someone before he put the glass down. That is how it ended up on the left side of the windowsill. So, I set it down.

Standing up straight, I leaned back against the stone that surrounded the window. The ledge was low and cut across the back of my knees. If my grandfather's trousers were snagged on the stone, and the snags were about mid-thigh, he must have caught them on the stones on the outside. But what does that prove?

I thought for a moment and then it hit me. If he caught his trousers on the inside of the window, one might assume he had sat down on the ledge and that maybe the fall was accidental. But, if the cloth was torn on the stones on the outside edge, he may have been pushed hard enough to have completely missed the stones on the inside ledge of the window!

I stood up straight, as if I was confronting some villain with hate in his eyes. I braced for the push that I knew would come, and with closed eyes waited for the inevitable outcome.

I felt a slight gust of air and heard a door swing open. Opening my tightly shut eyes, I saw Anita standing in the doorway with a puzzled look written across her face, one hand on the doorknob and the other on her hip. Slightly embarrassed but righteously redeemed at having discovered some new insight to the incident, I strode by her with my chin leading the way.

Cinghiale

There was a knock on the front door of the villa. The sound was too soft to wake me, but Ilsa rolled over and pushed gently on my arm to get my attention.

"Filippo," she whispered, "there's someone at the door." There was a thin reed of concern in her voice as I realized that she was probably thinking the same thing I was: too much of that "pleasure thing," and I bounded out of bed half expecting to find her father on the loggia. I pulled on some khaki pants and a wrinkled t-shirt and moved quickly to the door just as I heard another gentle knock.

Before reaching the threshold, I had already calmed down. If it was Ilsa's father, the knock would have been harder. So, without knowing who I'd face when I opened the door, at least I no longer feared finding an angry father.

Pulling the door open a bit and squinting into the mid-morning light, I saw Anita standing before me, her hands clasped in front of her. Her grim, unsmiling face told me that she knew I wasn't alone, but the twinkle in her eye told me she was pleased at the romantic turn in my life — she just wouldn't admit it.

"*Buona mattina,* Signor Filippo," she said with a respectful nod.

"*Buona mattina,*" I repeated, still squinting in the light.

"I am going to the market this morning. I need some food for the Castello, and I will be visiting the butcher. I can find some *cinghiale salame* there and I will prepare the risotto with *cinghiale* for you tonight."

Cinghiale salame, made from wild boar meat, was a specialty of Tuscany and one of my favorite foods. It was impossible to find in America and, when I had tried to bring some back after visits to the Castello, the U.S. Customs agents invariably took it from me. I had already treated myself to some of this delicacy since returning, but Anita's risotto con cinghiale was a dish to die for.

"You can invite your friend," she said, cocking her head in the general direction of my bedroom. Her smile put me at ease, and I knew there was no sense pretending. Besides, I knew Ilsa would never forgive me for depriving her of a chance at this dish.

"*D'accordo*," I said, with a half-guilty smile. "But we're going to Siena today and there's a salumeria there…"

Before I could finish, Anita chimed in. "*Sì, signore, La Casa Tardi!*" she said excitedly. She agreed that the *cinghiale salame* from that shop was the best in the area, and so I was assigned the task of picking it up for Anita's famous dish. I knew I better not screw it up, but I knew La Casa Tardi wouldn't let me.

I closed the door after getting very clear instructions from Anita about the level of seasoning — not too spicy — and the density of the meat — not too fresh and soft — and other more specific details to beware of. Returning to the bedroom, I saw Ilsa sitting up in bed, sheets pulled up only to her waist and her satiny olive skin otherwise bare for me to enjoy. Her hair cascaded down past her shoulders and rested on firm breasts, barely concealing them from my view. She smiled as she watched me watching her. With raised eyebrows and a flirtatious toss of her head, she silently invited me to spend a little more time in bed before tackling our assignment.

I stepped toward the foot of the bed, crawled on all fours past rumpled blankets we had kicked carelessly toward our feet in the night, and wrapped my arms around her. Her skin was warm and her kiss was moist. It would be a good day, I thought, as we rolled over together.

Antonina Frascati

Before departing for Siena, I stopped by the Castello to pick up some things. I sat down at the long, antique table in the main room to go over some papers.

Anita came in with a platter of fruit and pastries, and I was just taking a bite out of the sweet roll she had served me when she unexpectedly sat down at the table across from me. It was a bit unusual for her to join me like that, but with Nonno Filippo she had considered herself so much a part of the family that she joined him at the breakfast table almost as soon as she had served it.

With me it would have been different. Although she knew me well, I was more of a stranger to the house, and certainly a stranger to her routine. When she sat down, the action gave the impression of some importance, as if she needed this closeness to reveal some secret.

I looked up at her, a large hunk of sweet roll caught dangling from my mouth by the awkwardness of her stare, and waited for her to speak.

"Signor Filippo, do you know Antonina Frascati?"

Swallowing chunks of cinnamon and dough, I muffled an answer, "No. I don't think so." Then clearing my throat, "Who is she?"

"She works for Antonio Cosco, the exporter."

Then I recalled the attractive woman with the sensuous perfume. "Yes, now I remember. I met her at his office. What about her?"

"She was here. The day before your grandfather died."

Suddenly, Antonina's icy stare returned to me, and I wondered what business she had with my grandfather.

"She worked for Nonno Filippo's exporter. Could she have been here on business?"

"No. Signor Cosco always dealt personally with Signor Trantino."

"Then what?"

"I don't know, but after she left, your grandfather rushed out of the house looking very confused and upset. He went to the di Rosa vineyard and stood looking at the vines for a long time."

"And then what did he do?"

"He got in his car and drove away."

"Was it evening?"

"Yes. Why?"

"Well, I just wondered whether the Maserati had arrived. It was picked up by Riccardo that day."

"Yes, I remember," she answered. "No, he didn't drive the Maserati. I recall seeing him drive away in his old Fiat."

"What happened to Antonina?"

"She just left. I assume she returned to the Cosco house. You said you saw her there. Did you speak to her?"

"No. She seemed very cool to me. Perhaps she's that way with everyone, but she didn't say anything about coming to see Nonno Filippo."

"Perhaps such news would not be welcome at the Cosco house," Anita speculated.

"Perhaps."

A Blustery Day in Siena

The short route to Siena took us through narrow dirt paths cut between the vineyards of the Trantino property, then opened onto a paved road that shot straight toward the ancient city. The traffic was light but picked up a bit as we neared Siena, and we negotiated the traffic circles and blinking traffic lights with increasing delays.

Getting to Siena is easy; getting around in it is another thing. The old part of the city is well over a thousand years old and the streets were designed to handle only pedestrian traffic, and much less of that, in fact. Comfortably sized avenues often narrowed as they got closer to the center of town. Some thinned down so much that you suddenly find yourself stopped, squeezed between imposing walls on either side, impossible to move forward. Folding in the side-view mirrors sometimes helped, but even that is often not enough.

Combine this pervasive problem with blind turns, a confusing mishmash of one-way streets, and signs that don't always tell you what you need to know, and Siena is a veritable black hole for the average driver. I consider myself a better-than-average driver and had carefully chosen the Fiat for that day's journey since it was older and smaller than the Maserati, but I begged out of the challenge to negotiate the inner neighborhoods of Siena. I decided instead to park near the Chiesa di San Domenico, just outside the ancient walls, and proceed on foot.

Ilsa laughed at my muttered comments about twisting lanes of traffic and over-eager drivers, but she threw her arms around my neck and gave me a peck on the cheek when I surrendered our car to the public parking lot. From there, it was only a short walk to the Piazza del Campo anyway, and we would be able to sightsee along the way.

Siena holds delights for people of all ages, even those who live nearby and have had many years to behold her beauty. There are several prominent churches, including San Domenico, the oldest church and one-time basilica of the city. Its inner walls are now quite bare, although restoration efforts by archeologists have recovered some of the frescoes hidden behind centuries of paint. The green-and-white-striped Duomo of Siena is on the other side of the city and is regarded by many architects as one of the most amazing churches in all of Italy, if not Europe.

We passed by boutiques that showered us in the sweet smell of new leather from the racks of handbags and jackets displayed by the door. We marveled at the scent of roasted garlic and fresh herbs coming from the pizzeria further down the street, and window-shopped for jewelry in some of the old city's finest stores.

As we approached the center of town, the streets began to bend more, the two- and three-story buildings twisting around curves that were molded to the shape of the Piazza del Campo within, the main plaza that defined the Sienese personality.

It is in the Piazza del Campo that the Palio was run twice each summer. Thousands of people from all over the world descend on this otherwise placid city to witness a medieval spectacle unrivaled in excitement and passion. In the Palio, a race that pits the history and folklore of all the generations against each other, each neighborhood is represented by a horse and rider. For these two races dirt is trucked into Siena and spread on the stones of the Piazza, creating a dirt running track for the horse race. Thousands of people crowd the infield roughly defined by the asymmetric oval of the track, and thousands more hang from balconies of the buildings ringing the piazza.

There are rules for the race, but these are seldom observed. The riders are expected to use whatever creative means come to mind to ensure that their hated rivals fail — and that their own neighborhood wins. Kicking and strapping one another is common among the riders and seldom draws boos even from the opponents. There are even times that the rough tactics grow so extreme that a rider is pulled from a horse. In this case, the horse is still allowed to complete the race and could still be crowned the winner, but without a vengeful captain tugging at his flailing mane, it's unlikely such a horse would continue to run in this melee.

On the day Ilsa and I arrived in Siena, the scene at the Piazza del Campo was much more serene. With the heat of the summer tapering off and the tourists returning home, there were only small clumps of people meandering across the broad expanse of the city center. The fountain that trickled water was a polished white stone, and the bowl-shape contours of the piazza entertained the children who ran down one slope then up the other, only to return again on the next pass by their parents.

Stopping by a small bar on the perimeter of the Piazza, Ilsa and I bought some gelato, that staple of Italian life that may bring as many tourists back to this country as Rome itself. Strictly speaking, gelato is ice cream, but its textures are silkier, its flavors more intense, and its mouthfeel creamier than ice cream made elsewhere. The Italians whip less air into their product, raising the levels of texture and flavor, and serve this famous concoction in a mind-numbing gang of flavors. There's *cioccolato*, *caffé*, *limone*, *fragole*, and many more.

That day, since we were enjoying the blustery breezes that visit the city so often in late September, I didn't feel the need to cool off with a lemon, so I opted for the rich, creamy flavor of chocolate. Ilsa asked for two scoops, one of hazelnut and one of raspberry, and we strolled away rapt with the flavors and ecstatic that the taste of something special could be so much a part of life's happiness.

We talked about simple pleasures like these, how much it meant to be able to walk among the grand edifices of Italy while snacking on exquisite gelato. Ilsa laughed when I said that I seemed to talk about food and wine all the time, but then admitted with a girlish shrug that she did the same thing. This was something that was clear to me, once again since I'd resumed my life in Italy, that — in this country — food and wine were at the apex of the pyramid of pleasure. Italians all held pleasure as an important ingredient in life and thanked the heavens that they occupied a country so blessed with great art, superb music, classical architecture, and magnificent natural beauty. But they also regarded wine and food to be the greatest of all their achievements. The conquests of Caesar, the sculptures of Michelangelo, and the musical masterpieces of Puccini were all very wonderful, but it was the treasures Italians enjoyed as they sat down to the dinner table that they cherished most.

Another few blocks and another few shops and we were ready to sit down ourselves. The gelato refreshed us, but with all the walking, our appetites were once again renewed, and Ilsa and I scanned various menus posted in the windows of the restaurants along the streets to find one we'd like. After debating the options, we settled on a small trattoria just one street beyond the Piazza del Campo and embraced the cool air of the restaurant as we entered.

I ordered carpaccio and asparagus for starters and Ilsa asked for *pasta fagioli*. The carpaccio, a paper-thin slice of veal drizzled with the most wonderful extra-virgin olive oil paired nicely with the asparagus, which was grilled and served with balsamic vinegar sprinkled over shavings of Parmigiano Reggiano. Ilsa's white bean soup was succulent and very aromatic, as the fresh scent of herbs blended with the earthy aromas of beans and cooked garlic. As so many other dishes served in Italy, Ilsa's soup had a little stream of extra-virgin olive oil meandering across its surface that mixed in with the soup when she spooned it up. I watched with such apparent hunger that she offered me a spoonful and laughed when a bit dripped down my chin.

We ordered several more dishes, including risotto. I made Ilsa promise not to tell Anita I had risotto for lunch, but I watched a dish of it served to the next table and couldn't resist. For the main course, I had *pescespada capriciosa*, a broiled swordfish served with capers and green olives, with side dishes of grilled vegetables and pasta Bolognese. Ilsa was attracted to the pastas and resolved to have Tortelli di san Lorenzo. In this dish, pasta is stuffed with Parmigiano Reggiano, butter, salt, pepper and nutmeg and then topped with melted butter and more Parmigiano Reggiano.

Wine was served plentifully too, and before we knew it, we had consumed a full bottle. Pacing ourselves anew, we decided to finish the meal without any more wine.

It was a grateful respite from our long morning of touring, and reluctantly we emerged from the dimly lit restaurant into the bright sunlight of mid-afternoon. Walking through the Piazza del Campo back in the direction from which we had come, I asked an elderly man by the fountain if he knew the location of La Casa Tardi. He pointed across the Piazza and to the left, told me we would have to go two streets back, then turn left again, but it would be easy to find after that.

After continuing on our way, I confided to Ilsa that I had always found Italians to give terrible directions. "*Sempre diritto*," I told her I always heard, "always straight," waving my hand and pointing directly ahead of us. "What's that supposed to mean?" I asked her.

"Well," she chuckled, "a lot, maybe, and at the same time nothing. You see, the Italians think they should always give you the simplest directions, so they'll send you wide of the mark if they think that would involve fewer turns. In that way, *sempre diritto* could just be telling you that you're going to go straight, a lot, and not make many turns."

I looked at her sideways as if I didn't believe anything she was telling me, and she shrugged her shoulders and smiled broadly back at me.

A few streets later, negotiating the turns prescribed, we arrived at La Casa Tardi. A middle-aged woman behind the counter listened to our order for *cinghiale salame*, nodding her head as I repeated the instructions I had gotten from Anita, and kept nodding when I had completed my recitation. Then she stopped, furrowed her eyebrows, and considered me closely.

"*Lavora al Castello dei Trantini?*" she asked.

Not wishing to explain that I was from the Castello but didn't exactly work there, I simply nodded and said yes. But I wondered why she thought that.

"*Solo Anita*," shaking her head from side to side and throwing her palms up, and repeated herself, "Only Anita."

It was then I realized that Anita's instructions were so specific that this woman recognized them and probably also recognized that the *cinghiale salame* was destined for Anita's famous dish. The woman selected just the right salame, cut off two slices for us to taste and approve, then rolled it and another salame up together in brown paper and tied the whole thing with string. Handing it to me over the counter, she told me the total charge and put the money away in an open drawer at her waist.

Back to Cosco

On our way back to the estate, I swung toward the offices of the Cosco firm, deciding that I needed to ask one more question of Antonio.

He was in when we stopped by and admitted us readily to his office. I didn't notice his furrowed brow until he asked me where Antonina was.

"What?" I asked in astonishment.

"Where is she?" and now true concern showed on his face. "She always seemed so politely blasé, so uninvolved. Even when I took special pains to introduce her to the finer aspects of wine, she just shrugged her shoulders and went about her work. But ever since your grandfather's death, she has been as edgy as a cat on a fence. Then, this morning, she didn't show up for work."

"But why do you ask *me* where she is?"

"Because her anxiety seemed to increase since you visited. Did you know her before?"

"No," I responded defensively. "I had never met her before that day. But this morning, the cook at the Castello told me that Antonina visited Nonno Filippo the day before he died. When she left, he was in a very agitated state. Would you know anything about that, Signor Cosco?"

"No." Looking very puzzled, he continued, "But why would she visit Signor Trantino? I always handled the business affairs with him."

Ilsa was standing nearby, completely focused on the exchange, but clearly unsettled by the conversation.

"Unless it was a personal matter," I suggested.

"You don't think that Antonina had anything to do with your grandfather!" Then realizing his veiled insult, he added, "I'm sorry, Filippo, I didn't mean that the way it sounded. What sort of personal matter did you have in mind?"

"I'm not sure, but…"

Ilsa blanched at the thought.

Just then Mirelli walked through the open door and across the room.

"That would depend on what Signora Grana could tell us. Eh, Signor Trantino?"

I could tell that Mirelli's introduction of Raffaella Grana to this conversation caught Ilsa's attention.

"Yes," I had to answer, although I wondered why and how Mirelli had caught up to me. And I glanced at Ilsa to gauge her attention to all this.

"Signor Cosco," Mirelli continued, "you run a very profitable exporting business. And it seems that a large part of your profit derives from the wines of the Castello dei Trantino. Si?"

"Yes, but what does that have to do with this?"

"One day, your receptionist visits Filippo Trantino, uncommon behavior by your own admission, and the next day he is dead. Several days later, your receptionist disappears. Is there a common thread here, signore?"

"She is my receptionist, but she also works at the office of records for the province. Maybe her business with him stemmed from that association."

"Filippo Trantino dealt in wine," Mirelli said pointedly, "not records."

Cosco suddenly grew silent and, I must add, protectively uncooperative. After a few more questions, Mirelli turned to go and Ilsa and I followed, Mirelli considered would be the logical next step.

"Signor Trantino, you have been in contact with Signora Grana, yes?"

Ilsa's focus increased.

"Yes, I have. But from conversations with her, I doubt there'd be anything that could help us there."

Ilsa looked at me, somewhat accusingly, but more out of curiosity.

"Yes, perhaps. But I want you to talk with her again. See what you can find out. And let me know what she says."

Mirelli's assumption that I would comply with him, when in the beginning he was not even interested in investigating the death, rankled me. But I agreed.

Ilsa remained curious, but I avoided answering her questions on the ride back to the Castello.

Waking to the Sound of the Police

Franco Mirelli had no respect for sleep. He paid me an unwanted visit a few days later, before I even had time to gather my thoughts for the day. I suppose I should be glad Ilsa was not with me at that time, she having risen earlier to go to work, or else Mirelli would no doubt have been distracted and taken up even more of my time.

As we stood on the loggia, he launched into a description of his activities relating to the investigation.

"But, Signor Trantino, I thought you *wanted* the polizia to become involved?"

"I do. But must you call on people at such an hour?"

Sheepishly, he responded, "No, and I'm sorry if you've been inconvenienced. But I spoke again to Beppo."

"Beppo?"

"Yes, the man who sets up the bottles for your grandfather's tastings!"

"Yes, I know that. I have spoken to him also. But what did you ask him?"

"Whether he remembered seeing any mud on the carpet when he set up the tasting for that afternoon," said Mirelli.

"And he didn't. But did you know there was also no mud when my grandfather first entered the room."

"Beppo doesn't recall seeing any mud, that is true," said Mirelli, thoughtfully rubbing his chin, "but how do you know the other part?"

"Remember, Signor Mirelli. Nonno Filippo said everything has an aroma. If there was mud already on the carpet when he entered the room, he would have said something right away, to Anita, or Beppo, or someone."

"Well, how am I expected to know this?" Mirelli sounded defensive.

"You're not, Signor Mirelli. I know it because I know my grandfather. I will supply the intimate clues, but I do hope you'll supply the legal support."

"But of course."

"Signor Mirelli, what do you know about Antonio Cosco, the exporter, and the Giovanni della Francia house, especially the son Paolo?"

"Both are businessmen of high standing, though I'd avoid dealing with Paolo della Francia."

"Why?"

"Because he knows more about money than anything he sells to get it. He is a lonely man who sits in his counting room and makes up for the lack of human contact by surrounding himself with lire." Mirelli's reference to Italy's original currency, the lire, instead of the euro, which replaced it, made me smile.

"Do you think he might have had anything to do with my grandfather's death?"

Without a pause, as if being surprised by my line of questioning, Mirelli responded, "*No. Mama santa, no!* I couldn't imagine that man, weasel though he is, stooping to murder!"

"But why not? Should we exclude anyone from suspicion because he's too much a weasel to carry out such a terrible deed?"

"No. That would be no reason to exclude him," Mirelli said, shifting his weight from one foot to the other. "But don't you know about the contracts?"

"What contracts?" I asked.

"Before he gave his son final control over the house, Giovanni della Francia signed fifty-year contracts with most of his important customers. The Castello dei Trantini was among them, and the contracts bind the parties to unalterable conditions for the first twenty years, followed by negotiable terms for the succeeding thirty years."

"So, you're saying that Paolo was not in a position to change any of these conditions, by legal or illegal means, so he would have no reason to pressure any of the customers. Is that it?"

"*Sì*." At that, Mirelli straightened up, proud that he had added something to the investigation.

"Well, that does make sense, but I'll be honest with you, Signor Mirelli. Della Francia's attitude doesn't impress me much, and he seems every bit the type who would push an old man out a window."

"There you go again, Signor Trantino," he said with renewed confidence. "If solving these crimes was so easy, I'd be the commandant and you'd be a writer of fine mysteries."

I laughed at his summary and we shook hands. After he left, I was alone with my thoughts, standing on the loggia wearing only an old pair of jeans, with the first pangs of morning hunger just setting in. I looked up the hill toward the Castello, considered what little I had left in the refrigerator in the villa, and headed for the showers to dress more decently and go to the Castello so Anita could fix me some breakfast.

Vendemmia

The warm weather held up and the pickers were working feverishly to bring in the red grapes. At the beginning of each harvest season, the rows are checked individually to decide the best time to pick. But as the days wear on, after the vineyard manager declares first this row then that one ready for picking, the decisions become more general. At a certain point each autumn, Carlo, the vineyardist, smiles broadly and waves his arm in a great arc toward the vineyard, and says proudly, "*Sono pronti!*"

This declaration that all of the grapes are ready would be the final push, the long days of working in the field and in the winery, cutting literally tons of grapes from the vines, hauling them by gondola to the waiting crushers, then watching as the purple juice is pumped to the fermenters. There was more than enough work to do, and hiring more pickers didn't always satisfy the call for labor, so everyone on the estate was asked to pitch in.

During the final days of harvest, the winery's laboratories, osteria, and public store usually closed and the workers who normally tended glasses and corkscrews found themselves in the field. The actual harvesting of the grapes required some training, and we couldn't put unskilled workers to work doing that, but there were baskets of grapes to be emptied, trucks to be driven, and a lot of plain-old, hard manual labor at hand.

Everyone seemed to take it all with a cheery attitude. It's hard to suppress the utter joy of the harvest, especially among those who usually spend their days inside and seldom get that close to the fruit. But the days are long and, at times, it seems like they will never end. That's when nerves get frayed and patience begins to run out. For all his professionalism and maturity, Vito is often the first one to begin the serenade of complaints, shouting orders at workers who seem to be learning their new jobs too slowly.

I had been around the estate long enough to know all the jobs well. Besides, Nonno Filippo had told me countless times that the boss needed to know what the employees were doing. "It wouldn't be right," he would say with a serious look, "to ask someone to do something that you couldn't, or wouldn't, do yourself." So, for as long as I can remember, my grandfather would make me work alongside the others, moving from one assignment to another, until he felt I could run it all by myself.

I learned most of this before I had even reached a double-digit age and, even as a small boy, was always happy to join in the harvest. After my family moved to America, I couldn't come back for the grapes because I would be in school at that time. After finishing college, though, I resumed the routine and always visited at harvest — where I submerged myself in the miracle that was winemaking.

Morning came early on these days, as they are wont to do when the body is tired and the mind still preoccupied with yesterday's activities. I rose and pulled on old jeans and a t-shirt, then added a flannel shirt against the morning chill. I knew I'd doff the flannel as the sun rose in the sky, but I needed it for right now. I'd see less of Ilsa during this period, since there would be little time or energy left for fun until the harvest was over. So, to bear the parting, she spent the last night at the villa with me, and I could hear the hot-shower water slapping against the taut muscles of her body, echoing in the tiled confines of the shower. Pausing just a moment to bring up a clearer picture of her in my mind, I smiled, then shook it off, reminding myself of the work ahead.

Just then, Ilsa appeared around the corner using the towel to dry her hair rather than cover her body still moist from the shower, and I winced. She saw my pain, smiled seductively, then brushed too close to me on her way to the bedroom. "*Non oggi*," she said wagging her finger, "not today."

As I stepped out onto the loggia, Carlo saw me immediately and called me down into the vineyard. He had a small cluster of young men and women standing in a semi-circle in front of him, and he waved me over excitedly. As I entered his little ring of apprentices, I realized what he wanted.

"*Per favore, signore*," he said quickly, "I have more help for us since the vines are heavy with fruit. But I'm needed in the other field," he said pointing to some place in the distance. "Could you please explain to them how to properly cut grapes from the vine?"

"But can't we get some of our own employees who at least have been at the Castello for a while?"

One man stepped forward and took off his hat. "I know you're worried about our ability to do this, Signor Trantino," he began, "but my friends have worked vineyards before, just not here. I give you my word."

He was very respectful and even recognized me, so I relented a bit. Perhaps it was because he addressed me as Signor Trantino, as the true capo of the estate, rather than the diminutive Signor Filippo.

"Okay," I replied, "Let's see what you can do."

Carlo was already off on his Vespa scooter to parts unknown as the little group of pickers grabbed their shears.

"Let's start with this row and stick together. I'll make sure you know how to do it before moving on."

I would leave sooner than I planned, however, when I heard Riccardo swearing at a truck a few rows away.

"Signore," said the young man. "If you need to go, I will take care of this crew," he said sweeping his hand across the assembled workers.

"What is your name?" I asked.

"Rocco."

"Okay, Rocco," I said while taking quick glances at the workers and how they were doing so far. "Okay, thank you. I'll be back soon."

By the time I reached him, Riccardo was having a heated argument with the truck, and was waving his arms and directing his stares at it as if he expected the inanimate machine to respond. Just as I got close enough to ask what was wrong, the engine started up with a billowy puff of smoke, and Riccardo stood back and planted his fists on his hips in triumph. I was going to say something about arguing with a machine, and how it doesn't do any good, but I knew my comments would fall on deaf ears.

"Is there anything I can do for you, Riccardo?" I asked.

He gave me a funny look, and said, "No, of course not," as if he was surprised that I would interfere with his communing with machinery.

It went like that pretty much all day. In those rare moments that I had time to think, I thought about Ilsa, wondering if she too was somewhere out in the field or whether Vito had claimed her to help in the winery. I was stuck with my last mental image of her, though, with a towel wrapped around her head and nothing else to hide her glistening body. It was a thought I tried hard, and often, to put out of my mind.

After supervising the reassignment of some pickers who had finished one field and needed another, I returned to Rocco and his crew. They were working quietly along, clearing the vines of all usable grapes and depositing them gently into the waiting baskets. They talked very little and worked with great concentration. When I complimented Rocco on these workers, he grinned with satisfaction.

"They're from Portugal," he said. "They've had a bad season there this year, the vineyards have, and these people needed work."

They were so young, it was hard to believe they would be that good, but I thanked Rocco and tipped my hat to him as I returned to the field to see what else I could do.

Pickers were working smoothly down each row, and the trucks were transporting the fruit to the winery. I decided to hop on the next one and see what was going on under Vito's care. I had a secret hope that

I'd find Ilsa there, but I told myself the trip was more business than pleasure.

Just as the truck pulled up to the huge, auger-bladed crusher, I hopped to the ground. Inside the winery it was cool, kept that way by the shade and large ceiling fans that circulated the air, and also by the thousands of gallons of liquid stored within it. Liquid changes temperature more slowly than air, and when a building houses so much liquid, it alone can control the temperature of the air throughout the huge room.

I walked by the massive stainless-steel vats that were now commonplace at Castello dei Trantini. There were old wooden ones here for many years, but in a rare nod to modern technology, Nonno Filippo decided to replace the wooden fermenters with those made of stainless steel. In these new vats, the temperature of the fermenting juice could be carefully controlled, yielding more control over color extraction, tannin development, and the course of the entire fermentation. Grape juice heats up as the yeast converts the sugar to equal parts of alcohol and carbon dioxide. If the juice heats up too fast, or too much, the wine's flavors are damaged, sometimes so much that they're referred to as "cooked." If the temperature heats up too slowly, or too little, fermentation can "stick," meaning that it may fail altogether, and you end up with a very sweet, very un-wine-like beverage that's fit for nothing but fertilizer.

At first, Vito had scoffed at these new "tin cans," as he called them. But without ever admitting that they made his job easier, he came to like what he could make with them.

I saw Vito suddenly appear from behind the fermenter on the right, hopping over the hoses that snaked across the floor. Before I could even raise a hand in salute, he disappeared behind a large pump that sat atop a squat platform with wheels. The pumps served several stages of the process and it was common to move them from one area of the winery to another, as needed. I strode off in the direction of my last sighting of Vito, still intent of asking what there was for me to help with, when I ran smack into Elena, his sister.

"*Mi scusi,*" I said with a start, but she smiled and laughed at the brusque encounter.

"*Non c'é problema,*" she replied.

"Signora, your brother even has you working here today?" I asked with some amusement.

"*Si.* He said the grapes are the most important thing. He didn't say compared to what, but I think I know what he means." Again, she flashed a somewhat maternal smile at me, as if she understood men and their grapes as American women like to think they understand men and their toys.

"*D'accordo!*" I replied, then saluted with a tip of my hat and moved quickly on, drawn to a corner of the winery echoing Vito's unmistakable voice.

Long Days in the Vineyard

The pace and workload kept up like this for three more days. Workers moved around very little, focused only on the job at hand, but seldom took breaks and spent their days bent forward at the waist clipping bunches of purple orbs from the vines. I watched them and imagined the sore backs and sunburned necks that would trouble each at day's end.

The managers and others with supervisory responsibility spent more of their days dashing from one place to another but shared in the hard, physical labor whenever they were with a crew.

My hours spent picking grapes were few, but at night I registered aching knees from the crouching posture and aching arms from holding them up picking grapes all day. I was enlisted to help empty some of the lugs of grapes into the waiting gondolas, back-breaking work that smaller men seemed to accomplish through technique what I couldn't do with sheer muscle power.

My time spent in the winery had the single benefit of a cooler atmosphere, but it was here that the heaviest work often took place. Hoses needed to be moved from fermenter to fermenter, and even when empty they were enormous and unwieldy and proved difficult even for the experienced winery worker. As the fermenters filled, the piping that directed the flow of juice into the top hatch had to be moved, and scaling tall ladders in great leaps to assist in this task ultimately left my legs feeling wobbly.

One afternoon, when rain threatened, Vito called everyone out into the field in a frenzied attempt to get as much fruit off the vines as possible before the deluge ruined the vintage. But after a while, the clouds drifted away, the grey foreboding sky turned an azure blue once more, and we were able to breathe a sigh of relief.

But it was on that day that I saw Ilsa for the first time since that morning at the villa. I had just finished picking one row and turned the corner to join the crew on the other side. I saw her bent over toward the vine, concentrating with her eyes at the bunch that she cupped in her left hand, while her right hand snipped quickly at the stem. She carried out the motion with quickness and agility, as if she had years of practice snipping grapes from the vine, and I wondered again how long she had been involved in the Trantino enterprise.

I called out her name and, to my surprise, two women stood up to look at me. One was Ilsa, and I saw a broad smile sweep over her face, and just beyond her, also picking grapes, was her mother, who also smiled. Ingrid, Ilsa's mother, also looked the part of the peasant, sleeves rolled up and tanned arms slashing and snipping at the vines in a practiced rhythm. They both waved at me, then Ingrid resumed her work. The flash of recognition I detected from her showed that she expected her daughter to linger a moment longer, locked in a visual embrace, before returning to the work at hand. Ilsa did, and I enjoyed the brief moment together, even if it was from a distance.

I worked that row for a couple of hours, always two pickers away from Ilsa, but focused more on the grapes and on the muscles in my lower back that were getting stronger while they screamed out from the pain of repetitive movement. I began to hope for a call from Vito or Riccardo or Carlo, anyone to take me from the field, just as I knew that everyone on my left and right was probably thinking the same thing.

Nearing the end of the afternoon, as a cool breeze visited the vineyard, the pickers became more talkative. It relaxed everyone along the row as the level of conversation went from an occasional random comment about the heat to back-and-forth banter about the plans for the evening.

The cooler air allowed the sweat to dry on my forehead, leaving a sandy coating of salt that had escaped from my skin. The lower band of the baseball hat I wore was soaked through and resisted drying, but now the wetness left on the hat from my sweat served to cool my skin instead of irritate it. I straightened up, arched my back as far as I could, and let out a long, slow breath. Switching the clipping shears to my left hand for once, I shook my right hand, letting the muscles feel the freedom of having nothing to grip for a moment. A call to my right drew my attention, and, as I looked in that direction, I realized for the first time that Ilsa and her mother were long gone. They must have moved to another section while I was still concentrating on this one.

I looked again and saw that Vito was shouting in my general direction. He couldn't see me, the canopy of leaves on the vines was too dense for him to see where I was, but he was calling my name. I stood on my tiptoes and waved to signal where I was and, as I did that, Vito saw me, then waved vigorously at me to come over to him.

"Ah," I thought with relief. "A reason to leave the vineyard." Too bad it came as the air was cooling off, but, oh well.

I walked past pickers as I made my way to the end of the row. There were equal numbers of men and women, with more children than I would have expected. They were all wearing work clothes, many in flannels and tall socks that showed the dirt and grime of their daily routine. They also seemed unusually fit, physically strengthened by the work they did day in and day out. As I passed by these people, I thought about how essential they were to the process of making wine.

The grape pickers presented an interesting dichotomy. They needed certain skills, or else a winery owner wouldn't trust them in the vineyard. Yet they only worked a few weeks per year. That accounts for the migrants from Portugal that Rocco had in his crew. When there are grapes to be picked, they need to go pick them or else forfeit the money that could be had at that time of year. Still, they only had a precious few weeks, or at most two months counting white and red grapes, to earn this money. With this seasonal, semi-skilled workforce, the winery could harvest all its fruit on time and make its annual share of wine; without the pickers, the fruit would never get to the winery and would die a desiccated death on the vine.

Pondering these things, I began to appreciate the pickers all the more, and the crew chiefs who shepherded them. I resolved to find Rocco after this harvest was over and put him on our payroll.

I cut through the access road in the middle of the vineyard and headed in Vito's direction. As I reached the roadway, I was still watching the pickers when a voice rang out in my ears.

"Filippo!" it shouted. "Filippo! *Attenzione!!*"

I turned to my right and saw that I was in front of a large flatbed truck, filled to overflowing with baskets of grapes and barreling down on me out of control. I leapt into the drainage ditch beside the last row of grapevines, falling awkwardly, and looked back to see Riccardo in the driver's seat. He was waving his left hand out the window in a gesture of apology, with a look on his face as is to say that he was sorry but it wasn't his fault. A hundred yards later, the truck faced an incline and slowed to a stop by virtue of gravity.

"You have to watch out," said Ilsa, standing over me next to the vines. She was smiling and had her hands on her hips in an almost disapproving posture, and she seemed less concerned with my safety than surprised that I would be so careless.

I stood up, brushed myself off, and said, "What's wrong with him?"

"Who, Riccardo?" she asked. Then looking off in the direction of the runaway truck, she said, "Oh, Riccardo just hasn't had time to fix the brakes in that one yet."

When I finally reached Vito, he, too, was laughing at me. But he hid his smile behind his leathery right hand and asked me to come with him to the winery. He avoided the scooter that Carlo preferred, but climbed into an old Fiat with dusty windows and a rearview mirror that dangled from the windshield as he drove.

At the winery, the cool air I had sought earlier that day was less inviting, if only because the work was nearing an end and the heat had receded. Vito showed me the fermenters, how most of them were already full, and how he planned to manage the remaining grapes coming in from the field.

"We've had a very good year, Signor Filippo," he said, slapping the side of one of the vast stainless-steel fermenters with affection. "We have most of the crop in already, good reports for weather tomorrow and the next day, and enough pickers to get the fruit that remains on the vine."

"When will we be finished?" I asked.

Vito rubbed his chin and stared intently down at the floor. "Two more days, I think. Maybe then," he said with studied finality.

I told him I had some business in town and, if the work was going so well, perhaps I could take tomorrow off to manage the other affairs.

"*Certo*," Vito said. Then he added, "Since we have done so much, perhaps I should let some of the other workers off to return to their usual routine?"

He said this with a slight look, an imperceptibly subtle twinkle in his eye I took to mean he was referring to Ilsa. I didn't want to guess at his meaning of "usual routine," but I nodded yes to his suggestion.

Later that night, I made my way slowly back to the villa, then climbed the steps up to the loggia on the second floor. From this vantage point, I could see most of the best vineyards in the estate's possession. I could still see some pickers among the vines, but the light was nearly gone and there was little left for them to do that evening. I rested my hands on the stone wall in front of me and leaned out a bit to stretch my back. As the sun set on the horizon, once again drawing the lights out in Siena to the left, I drew in a deep breath and enjoyed, truly enjoyed, this life as a winery owner.

Sitting down on the chair to relieve my aching muscles, I heard the sound of gravel crackling under the rhythm of someone's footsteps. In a moment, Ilsa appeared at the bottom of the steps, pausing just a moment while she looked at me, as if she needed an invitation to ascend. My smile must have sufficed, because she strode purposely up the stone steps and stood before me.

She could have been a cover model for *Harvest News*. She wore the grape-stained shirt and old jeans of a field hand, tall leather boots that had obviously served her for many years, and a sweat-stained scarf around her neck. But her skin glowed, her eyes twinkled, and, in her hand, she held out a bottle of the Castello dei Trantini Chianti. It was not a night to appreciate something more sophisticated, and Ilsa knew this, so she managed to secure a bottle of our simple, everyday wine and came bearing it and two glasses in her hands. Setting all this down on the table, she pulled a corkscrew from her back pocket and proceeded to open the bottle, all the while smiling at me.

It wasn't as if I didn't have wine, glasses, and a corkscrew in the villa, and she knew this too. But we sat side by side for a long time, too tired to talk, but sipping the wine and enjoying just being near each other.

I don't even remember how I got to bed that night, but awoke the next morning lying on top of the sheets, fully clothed, as was Ilsa lying next to me. We were obviously too tired to do anything, but at least made it that far to sleep on the soft, inviting mattress.

Back to Radda

I returned to the Piazza Vecchia in Radda and sought out Raffaella Grana. I rang the bell on the doorjamb at the street level and waited until she answered the intercom. Waiting for a response, I watched the men who sat at the cafe across the piazza from where I now stood. She answered the call and, when my voice revealed who I was, her voice became spirited and she encouraged me to come up to her apartment without delay.

As I ascended the two flights of old stone steps to her flat, I saw the door opening and light cascading down upon me. She stood in the doorway, illuminated from behind by the large chandelier in the living room, with an uneasy smile on her face. As I made it to the top of the stairs, she embraced me and led me inside. She seemed so anxious to have a visitor, especially one so close to the one she had just lost, that I hesitated to change the mood.

"Antonina Frascati is missing," I blurted out.

"Who is this person?"

"Antonina visited Nonno Filippo the day before he died. Only hours before he visited you the last time."

"Is she pretty?"

Then I realized that in my haste, I had opened a discussion not knowing where it would lead.

"No, I'm sorry, that isn't what I meant." I hoped. "She must have had some business with him. They discussed something at length and, when she left, Nonno Filippo was very upset. The next day he came to visit you. Can you remember anything else about what he said that day?"

"No, Filippo. I'm sorry, but I can't." She seemed to be racking her brain for answers and, not finding any, punished herself.

"Stop for a moment, Signora Grana, and think. Pretend I'm not here. Was there anything that he said that might give us a clue to what bothered him?"

"No. Except...except, but that couldn't mean anything!"

"What? I'll take anything now."

"He kept saying, 'Names. Names!' And then sometimes he would say, 'I should have figured it out!' What does that mean, Filippo?"

I sat wide-eyed and dumbfounded. I had no idea what those words would mean. I squeezed my eyes shut in concentration and tried to imagine what Nonno Filippo would have been thinking when he said those words. And I failed.

"I don't know, Signora Grana. The words may be important, but I can't begin to imagine why. Was there anything else? Please, I'm sorry to press you like this, but you must try to remember."

"No, Filippo. I do not mind. But now I am certain that there was nothing else. The other time you visited and you asked me these questions, I was unsettled. But after thinking about it, I remember only those words from the night Filippo saw me last. He was so obsessed, those words were all he uttered, they were all he could think about. But I do know that he was so upset about the information he had that he didn't want anyone to know about it. He even cautioned me not to let anyone know what we had discussed."

Then, breaking down in tears, she added, "He said that even if something happened to him, the Trantino name was more important. 'Don't do anything to ruin the Trantino name,' he said. He didn't say anything more, and soon he left."

I knew that Nonno Filippo must have returned at that point to the Castello. He normally began his wine tasting at 4:00, and if there was any variation in that routine I would have already heard. As I guided the Maserati down the back roads from Radda to Salina and then to the Castello, I let memories guide my mind.

I tried to imagine my grandfather in an agitated state, one that I had never seen him in, though one I could at least imagine. The wine library always seemed to put him at ease, and I suppose that no matter what bothered him, once he returned to the Castello, he would, like me, be unable to suppress a smile and a welcome embrace. Then he would be happy, even if only for a while, and he could ascend the stairs to the wine library, enjoy his ritual of testing and tasting wines, and forget about the things that troubled him.

My eyes jerked open as I realized that I was still driving the Maserati and had pictured the previous scene with eyes closed. Settling my nerves and returning to my thoughts, I had to admit that it was true. No matter what problems plagued my grandfather, when he returned to the security of the Castello, especially the wine library on the second floor, they all seemed like so much sand in the wind. That was what made the shove out the window all the more sinister. It happened in the place Nonno Filippo felt most safe.

A Long Morning

Ilsa returned to the villa that night and we slept long into the morning. The windows were open during the night, letting in the crisp cool air, against which we huddled under blankets for comfort. Streaks of sunlight were peering through the branches of the tree outside our window. I opened my eyes to see that the sun had risen to about ten o'clock, then rolled over to see that Ilsa was already awake and beaming back at me.

"*Buon giorno, Signor* Trantino," she said. Ilsa was only the second person at the Castello to address me as Signor Trantino, and this caused me to reflect on my potential role at the Castello dei Trantini.

"*Buon giorno, signorina,*" I replied, pulling myself closer so that I could kiss her.

Ilsa buried her head a little deeper into my neck, and I stroked her hair. A rap at the door brought us out of the moment, and I slipped on an old pair of pants to see who it was.

"*Buon giorno, signore,*" said Elisabetta, standing at the door with a grocery bag in each hand. "I knew you were very busy the last few days and probably would be out of food, so I brought you this." She held up both bags, and I could see — and smell — that they were filled with fruit, fresh coffee grounds, and fresh bread. She swept past me without being invited in and nodded a courteous "*buon giorno*" to Ilsa who was standing behind me. It seems that Ilsa's presence beside me was being taken for granted around the estate; it even seemed that some of the people at the Castello dei Trantini were counting on her to settle my plans on whether to stay or go.

Elisabetta left as quickly as she had come, but not before setting the table on the loggia with some of the food in her bags and setting the coffee machine to go. This left Ilsa and me a chance to talk once again, a simple pleasure we'd been denied now for so long, too long.

"You're quite an expert with the shears," I volunteered, showing how impressed I was.

"*Sì*, Filippo, but you don't know so much about me."

"Well, tell me, then."

She looked up at me past long eyelashes, then began her story. "I have worked at the Castello dei Trantini for as long as I can remember. When I was a little girl, I picked the grapes. When I was about fifteen, I learned to help Vito in the labs."

"Ah," I said with raised eyebrows. "That's where you were most of the week. In the winery."

"*Sì*. Vito has recognized my ability in science. He was the one who said I should go to the university and study botany. He encouraged me from the time I was very young to learn about scientific instruments, plants, and animals. He was, what do you say in English, my 'mentor?'"

"Yes, your mentor."

She told me more about Vito's teaching her, and how he helped her to understand things about science and technology to prepare her for her studies in the university. As I listened to Ilsa, I tried to picture brusque, business-like Vito kindly attaching himself to a budding young scientist and coaxing her toward a career in science. Vito never married and had no children to guide, but he seems to have taken an interest in Ilsa as his adopted child.

"Is that the reason you went to go to the university to study science? Is Vito your model?"

Ilsa looked down, a bit embarrassed, but when she looked up again, she was full of the same confidence and tenacity that I recognized in her from the first.

"*Sì*, that is the reason. And at the university I learned a lot, and I plan to apply my education to improvements in the vineyard."

It was intriguing to consider whether Ilsa meant "the vineyard" in a broad, general sense, or whether she meant "the vineyard" that lay just outside our door, the di Rosa vineyard.

We talked as long as the coffee held out, then I knew it was time that I showered and got going. I was supposed to meet Santo and Rita for lunch but wanted to make my rounds of the vineyards first to get a sense of the damage that might have been done during the harvest. Nonno Filippo always reminded me that picking grapes is the most interesting part of winemaking, but he also warned me that droves of sometimes unfamiliar workers could damage the vines or the stakes and cross-wires that supported the fruit. I wanted to drive around the perimeter of at least the di Rosa vineyard this morning to see if everything was all right.

At around two o'clock, I made my way to Carlino d'Oro and settled into a table alone. Santo and Rita soon arrived, and we started off with a liter of the house wine.

Up until that point, I had only discussed some of the investigation with them, and I was sure they wanted to know more. They began to query me as soon as they arrived. At first, I didn't like what seemed to be their implication that I had not done enough, considering that they hadn't contributed much to the cloak-and-dagger work. But I relented, realizing as they did that the work must go on if an answer were to be found, and given this tragedy happened before harvest made it crucial to continue before more time passed.

"I'm sure if you knew the murderer by now, you'd tell us, Filippo," was Rita's opening salvo.

"Yes, you know that. But no, I do not know who it is. I have some thoughts, and some leads, but no clues as to the identity of the person."

"You know," Santo joined in, "as tracks cool, they become harder to trace."

His analogy conjured up images of the Old West, and I took offense that he would use such an American phrase to challenge my progress. But I avoided a confrontation.

"I've been here for several weeks, but I have heard nothing about a reading of a will. Didn't Nonno Filippo have one?"

"No," Rita responded, "but he always said that his position as capo should pass on to his first son's first son, his namesake — you. Which was strange."

"What do you mean?" I asked, probably sounding more defensive than I should have. "It's common to leave such matters to one's namesake."

"But his grandfather left everything to his last surviving grandson, Nonno Filippo, rather than his first grandson and namesake, Vito."

"So?" I asked. "His first grandson, Vito, died in an automobile crash. Of course Nonno Filippo would have been next in line."

"But, no," said Rita, wagging a finger to dispute my claim. "Our great-great-grandfather, Vito, stipulated in his will that Vito would be passed over and the role of capo would go to Nonno Filippo, even before the accident."

I thought for a moment and then asked, "How long has the Trantino family actually owned the Castello?"

"Since before its current reputation," Santo said proudly. "This family built the business up from the ground. We restored the Castello, tilled the land, planted the vines, and built a reputation unlike any other in Tuscany."

"Yes. I share your family loyalty. But how long has it been called the Castello dei Trantini?"

"It really started more than a century ago," said Rita.

"Our great-great-grandfather, Vito Trantino, farmed the land for years for some loathsome land baron who insisted on growing cash crops." Santo explained. "After a time, Vito Trantino saved enough money to buy the land he had toiled over and converted it to vineyards. Within the first ten years, he had made enough money to restore the old castello, plant some more acres of vines, and ten years after that he was trading with some of the finest markets in Europe."

"Let's not forget his wife, Elena Trantino," Rita added. "A lot of the credit should go to that woman who pushed Vito to buy more land."

"Yes," Santo remarked with a broad smile, "but let's also remember that Vito married Elena in part because her father owned the adjoining vineyards!"

The blood drained from my face. It dawned on me so suddenly that I felt that I myself might die before I could prove what had just come to me. The others stared at me with worried looks, but as soon as I had regained the strength to move, I leaped from my chair and shouted.

"That's it! Names! I should have known!"

I rushed from the room, and before Santo and Rita could follow, I was already in the Maserati zooming down the lane toward Casteln-uovo Berardenga.

The Records

I sat in the office of records, pouring through musty documents older than me, some older than my grandfather. I knew what I was looking for but couldn't find it. Just as I felt I was drawing closer to it, a whiff of a familiar perfume caught my attention. I turned quickly around and looked directly into a voluptuous female torso. Letting my eyes drift upward, I saw Antonina looking down at me.

"You know, don't you," she said, without it sounding like a question.

"Yes, but I didn't realize it until Santo reminded me of the Italian custom of naming children. When I reflected on the words Signora Grana repeated, I put it together. I know that..."

"Shhh. Not here," she said with a finger to her glossy red lips. "Come with me."

I closed the book that I had been so carefully researching, knowing in my heart that the information from Antonina would be enough to prove my suspicions, and I followed her out the door.

We stood behind the Cosco offices, in a narrow street so common in Italy, one which suddenly seemed so private, so removed from the life I had known in Italy. We were going over the family tree, naming each member of every generation, and I realized that Antonina – not a Trantino – had memorized the order and relationship of everyone she had found in the office of records.

Without pen or paper, I could visualize it all, and when we grew quiet, Antonina knew that I had seen in this genealogy what she first saw and reported to Nonno Filippo.

Understanding It All

I left Antonina and walked slowly to my car, recalling her words.

She had discovered some information that she felt would be important for my grandfather but, after delivering it to him, she was terrified at the way he received it. Then, when he was found dead the next day, she too feared for her life. She maintained her composure and continued with her normal routine until I showed an interest in proving the death to be a murder. The renewed interest of the police was the final straw, and she hid herself as protection against the person who killed my grandfather.

When I arrived at the Castello, I walked straight up to the wine library, walked across the room, and opened the window, then sat down at the desk at the far end of the room. I contemplated the telephone for a long time, finally lifting the receiver and dialing the winery.

"Ask Vito to come to see me in the wine library," was all I said.

As the footsteps announced his arrival, I stood up and faced the door.

"Vito. Please come in."

The old man looked sheepishly at me and then the color drained from his face.

"Please don't track in any mud from the vineyard," I added directly.

Vito looked at his feet and protested that he would never bring dirt into Signor Trantino's wine library.

"Not unless you were in a hurry, or your disposition made you unmindful of your dirty shoes, eh?" I added.

Vito was standing quite still with arms by his sides, obviously not knowing whether to move or speak.

"You've been here for a long time, Vito, haven't you? When were you first hired?"

"I don't remember, Signor Filippo, but it was when I was still a little boy. I used to work in the vineyards for your great-great-grandfather when your grandfather and I were both boys. Later, I became the winemaker."

"Yes, so I've heard, Vito. And your sister, Elena, did she ever work here?"

"Elena? No, I'm quite sure she never worked here, Signor Filippo."

I walked around the desk so I could get a better look at Vito in the light.

"Vito, Nonno Filippo did not fall out the window. He was pushed."

There was no reaction from him, so I pressed on.

"Nothing made sense until Santo said that our great-great-grandfather, Vito Trantino, had bequeathed everything to his last surviving grandson. His first grandson, named Vito after him, died in an automobile accident."

Still no reaction from Vito.

"So, he had only one surviving grandson, Filippo, who took over the winery and ran it for these many years," I said.

Still no reaction from Vito, who just stood there looking at the tasting table and shifting glasses back from its edge in an unconscious motion. "You're familiar with the naming sequence most Italians use, aren't you, Vito?"

His silence gave me the go-ahead to continue.

"In Italy, there is a particular order for every child's name. The first son is named after the father's father, the first daughter is named after the father's mother, the second son is named after the mother's father, and so on. Right?"

Silence.

"Well, it occurred to me that it was quite odd that Vito and Elena Basiglio, as the first children born to your parents, would have names that fit the sequence for my great-great-grandparents. It's almost as if you were the children of Vincenzo Trantino, the grandchildren of Vito and Elena Trantino, the brother and sister of my Nonno Filippo."

Now Vito's face was white.

"Names such as yours might be confused with those of the grandson and granddaughter of Vito Trantino, who in this case, would be the heir to the Castello dei Trantini. So, I went to the office of records to check your birth certificates. As it turns out, Antonina was there to intercept me. Through her I found out that your mother, Carmella Giglio, married Riccardo Basiglio two years *after* your younger sister Elena was born. So Riccardo Basiglio was probably not your father."

Vito stood rigid before me, then a low wail escaped from his lips.

"Signor Filippo, you do not understand. You know only facts. You do not know the truth behind the facts."

"The truth is that your mother, Carmella Giglio, and my great-grandfather were in love, and that love produced two children. Carmella loved Vincenzo so much that she chose to name the children she bore him according to the tradition. So, the first-born son was named after his father's father, Vito, and the first daughter was named after his father's mother, Elena. She carried this love with her until she married Riccardo Basiglio. Then the first Vito Trantino, to punish his son for fathering children outside his marriage, bequeathed the entire estate to his last *surviving* grandson. Which might very well have been you, except for my late grandfather's longevity!"

At this point, I felt I was losing control, facing the man who had pushed my grandfather out the window to his death. But Vito's whimpering stopped me.

"Signor Filippo, you still do not know all the facts. I never knew these things before. Antonina told your grandfather that she had discovered the birth records and the importance of this information to the will that Vito Trantino had written. Filippo gave me this information.

"The next evening, I went to the wine library to talk to him, to determine what this meant for us. When I had realized who my father was, and that I had worked for so many years as a hired hand at the estate that I was family to, I was upset. Filippo was standing where you are now, Signor Filippo." Looking behind me, I moved instinctively away from the window.

Vito was acting guilty, but his story seemed a bit detached and mechanical.

"I was angry," he halted, "angry about being deceived for so long, so we argued. Filippo stood with his back to the window, to the scene he loved so much for so long. He said that he hadn't known these things he was telling me, and that he wanted me to know as soon as he found out. That we had the same father. I was angry because I had been only an employee for so many years, living in the cottage behind the main house, while Filippo lived in the Castello.

"Filippo was upset and confused." Here, Vito paused, as if he was unsure of what to say next.

"Filippo confronted me, and I guessed I lashed out. I didn't mean for anything to happen. We were brothers – and suddenly that seemed to be a factor in our argument – but that didn't calm us.

"I moved toward him, and Filippo stood from the windowsill, waving his arms as he said, 'We must solve this.' I reached out, pointing my finger at him to make a point and he waved his arm to brush me away. He stumbled backward and, in an instant, he was gone. I think," Vito paused again, "he stood so suddenly and lost his balance, and fell backward through the window. He was gone."

Vito's story fit the facts, but it was said without emotion. It seemed impossible to believe.

Just then, the door swung open and Elena burst into the room. The three of us looked at each other with a mixture of surprise, suspicion, and fear.

"Get out," Vito said. "You don't belong here."

I watched their body language closely, and I knew right away that Elena would not obey her brother's command.

"*Che fai?*" she said to Vito. "What are you doing?"

"I said get out," he repeated.

Elena looked at me, then back at Vito. I decided not to interfere, knowing that there was something more I was about to learn. But it was obvious to me that Elena knew what Vito had done.

Elena strode across the room toward me, with all the confidence of someone who knows the truth, and knows their fate.

"He's lying. I killed Nonno Filippo," she said, and Vito's chin sagged. Her announcement may have been intended to be forceful, but her lip trembled, and her voice was tinged with a soulful remorse.

I let her continue.

"Vito told me what Nonno Filippo had revealed, and we argued. I told him he should inherit the Castello dei Trantini, he had slaved at the winery for decades, and he was only considered a hired hand. I told him he was the rightful heir and should claim it.

"Vito was unsure how to proceed. I wasn't. After agonizing about it all night and into the next day, I told Vito something had to be done. We argued about the right path so I left him standing in the roadway so I could do something. It was a little after four o'clock so I knew that Nonno Filippo would be in the wine library. I went there to ask him – no tell him – what was going to happen now.

"I entered the room and saw Filippo standing by the window. I demanded that he recognize Vito as a member of the family. Of course, I knew that this made me a member of the Trantini clan also, but that didn't matter to me.

"Filippo sat on the windowsill and wiped his brow, he was so upset by our argument," she continued. "But I was not deterred. The years of deprivation, of not knowing who our father was, and of suddenly feeling like we had lived here, that Vito had been employed here, only because we were the accidental offspring of the 'master' made the blood rise to my face. I lost control, and I moved closer to Filippo sitting on the windowsill."

Elena stood with tears running down her cheeks, looking directly at me as if she could redeem herself for the act she was about to recount.

"My voice rang out and my arms flailed, and suddenly I was upon him. I did not push him, but I felt as though Filippo was responsible for everything, and for Vito being deprived of his rightful inheritance. As I jabbed a finger in his chest, he moved as if to defend himself. In the act of standing quickly, he lost his balance.

"The window sills," she cried, "they're so low here." Elena looked mournfully at the stone ledge of the window, as if it could help her recover the loss. "He just fell out!" she cried. "He just fell out!"

Now she was sobbing. The picture was crystal clear to me, and unfortunately too clear for Elena. As she continued, Elena explained that her brother had run into the room moments too late.

Vito mumbled, "I saw her standing at the windowsill, in shock. I looked out and saw Filippo on the stones below. All I could think of was to get her out of there, get both of us out of that room until we could think things through."

Vito had chosen to take the fall for his sister, deciding that he could shoulder the blame and let her escape. But Elena wouldn't let him.

Just at that moment, Ilsa appeared in the doorway, looking from me to Elena to Vito.

"*Che cos'é?*" she asked.

Striding purposefully past her and taking her by the wrist, I said only, "I'll tell you later," and we left.

Whose Inheritance Is It Now

Afterward, I didn't want to see or talk to anyone. I had drawn Ilsa out of the wine library but couldn't bring myself to explain what had taken place. I told her to go home and wait for me to call.

I returned to the villa and tried to think through all this. Standing on the loggia in the fading sunset, I heard the telephone ring.

"*Pronto*," I said, putting the receiver to my ear.

"Hi, son," came my father's voice.

What bad timing, I thought. I needed to talk to him, I wanted to talk to him, but I had no idea what to say. His first question didn't help.

"Phil, what have you decided about your inheritance?"

My inheritance was now, technically, Vito's inheritance, since he outlived Nonno Filippo. But it was wrong, in so many ways. I now thought I understood everything, but at the same time felt like I understood nothing.

What was I supposed to say? That I was – sort of – next in line, but that Vito, whose sister had just eliminated the only person standing in the way, was more likely the legal heir to the Trantino estate. I considered another version: that I would inherit the estate, but Vito and Elena would go to prison. Well, that wasn't going to happen because Vito didn't do anything other than protect his sister. If Elena went to prison, and Vito was allowed to go free, wouldn't he be the heir? And if Vito convinced a judge that his confession was true, he would go to prison and Elena, well, Elena would die of a broken heart.

"Son, are you there?" I heard over the telephone line.

"Yeah, um, hmmm," I stammered. "It's a bit complicated, Dad. Can I call you back tomorrow?"

Rethinking It

The next day I had to return to the business of wine, but I couldn't forget what I had just learned. I experimented with different versions of the fatal events.

Elena was in the wine library when Nonno Filippo fell out of the window. No, wait, that's too innocent for what she did. Elena was in the wine library and pushed Nonno out the window.

That didn't sound right either. Elena argued with Nonno Filippo and a horrifying accident occurred. That's what happened. I would end my investigation by explaining that to those who asked, like the recently interested Captain Mirelli. And to my family.

And Vito would inherit the Castello dei Trantini. My chest heaved, and then fell, at the thought.

Later that afternoon, I called my dad as promised.

"Phil, you were very distracted yesterday. Did Santo and Rita get to you? Do you think that my father's death was anything but an accident?"

Finally, a question I could answer with complete honesty.

"It was an accident." It was then that I began to conceive of a way out of this dilemma.

Fixing Things

That evening I walked down to the winery. Vito told me that he felt the Castello dei Trantini had given him a chance to become someone, and he had worked hard through the years to take advantage of that opportunity. This made him feel like he belonged. He was surprised by the news that he was actually a Trantino but horrified by what had happened when Elena confronted Filippo. "My brother," Vito said with a mixture of love and remorse. He didn't want some indiscreet secret buried in the city's old record books to change what he had become, what he had accomplished as the winemaker of this fine estate.

Then, saddened a bit, he talked about how he never married. He wanted to have a wife and family, but just never got around to it. His mood changed a bit when he joked that perhaps it was because he was just too short, or not good-looking enough. Then he dropped back into his sullen despair.

After a while, Vito returned to the subject of the present. He said he didn't want the winery or the Castello. He was too old to become someone new, and he had no son or daughter to pass the wealth on to.

He also pleaded with me not to let it be known that Elena was in the room when the accident occurred. "No one will understand, we will never be able to live in this area if anyone thinks we were involved with the death of the sainted Nonno Filippo."

Then he said, "Filippo, you are my son, you are my heir. I taught you how to grow grapes and to make wine. If I were the capo and

I died, you would inherit this estate anyway," and he completed his statement with a grand sweep of his arms, indicating everything that surrounded us.

Ilsa sought me out that evening. Assuming I would be settled into the loggia, she easily located me there.

I wanted to spare her the details, but Ilsa was so much a part of my life by that point that I couldn't keep it all from her.

We sat facing the vineyard, sipping thoughtfully at the tumblers of Trantini wine before us, as I slowly explained to her what I had found out. She asked first what would happen to Elena, and I said I was still trying to figure it out.

Of particular interest to both of us were Vito's feelings about his inheritance. Ilsa was respectful and attentive, as always, but on this particular evening I could sense a special care expressed in her questions. It was like her affection for me – dare I say love – was trying to reach out to comfort me.

"Santo and Rita said the muddy boot prints were a man's," she said, more a question than a statement.

"I wondered about that, especially when I first thought that Vito was the one who confronted Nonno Filippo. Entering that room, even to have an argument, Vito would have shed his boots. But when I found out that Elena was there first, and Vito was rushing up to the wine library to stop her, he wouldn't have even thought about his boots."

It was all so clear.

"Vito tracked in the mud," I continued, "which supported his own lie and led us to the search for a man. Ironically, if he had not muddied the rug in the wine library, there would have been no evidence of another presence in the room, and this might all have gone down as an accident."

"And would he then have claimed his inheritance?" Ilsa asked.

Not being caught up in a murder investigation might have freed Vito from the guilt, and revealing his heritage to gain the Castello dei Trantini might have been worth it.

"I don't know," I said.

After my long description of the things that had happened and the impact it had for me, we just sat in silence for more than an hour. Slowly, and silently, we rose in unison, collected the wine glasses and now-emptied bottle and, depositing them in the kitchen sink, walked without purpose to the bedroom for a fitful night's sleep.

The Crush

The vines were nearly picked clean, and the work was shifting to the winery. There, the fermenters continued to fill up, Vito's staff walked around the building with notepads and pencils monitoring the progress of the juice, and hoses were slowly disappearing, to be stored away for a few weeks until they were needed again.

I longed to forget what I knew, to focus only on the grapes on the vine, but I couldn't. I worked, but I was distracted.

Vito supervised most of this activity but, by now, was spending more of his time on the catwalk platforms that laced the air above the fermenters and the winery's remaining old wooden vats. From this place, he could peer into the vats, using sight, smell, and, sometimes, taste to decide how well the wine was proceeding, and walk to the next vat, and the next, along the platform without having to descend a ladder and scale back up another one. It was like a separate floor to the winery, but one with only ladder-like walkways, that circumscribed the working platform for Vito and his assistants. Whenever he was finished using his natural talents to check on the wine, one of his assistants would pull out a few clear glass jars to draw samples and conduct a more scientific assessment.

Many of the employees who had been pressed into service in the vineyard were now gathering in the winery. They weren't needed in this phase; in fact, handling fermentation was considered the most difficult and specific process in winemaking, and Vito would have only allowed his trained staff to participate. But the workers gathered for other, more human, reasons.

I sensed that many now spent their time in the winery because they found themselves suddenly without work after many days of toiling from sunup to sunset. Others were drawn to the dim, cool confines of the winery for more mystical reasons. For winemaking was still revered as an almost mystical event. Grapes turned into wine on their own; the mixing of the fresh fruit with the wild yeast that blooms naturally on their skins would result in wine even without the intervention of human contact. Centuries of practice and scientific research has refined the process and, perhaps, given the world better wines, but nature is still the true winemaker.

As I now watched people gathering in the gaping doorway of the winery, waiting for a celebration of the end of the grape picking, I listened to their pleased laughter and mingled conversations. Through this ordinary hum, I came to appreciate — once again — the almost divine power of wine to bring people together. It wasn't just the drinking of it that made the difference. It was every moment in the process from vine to wine. It was the unity created by working side by side under a blazing sun, young and old getting dirty and sweaty together. It was the heady perfume of the grape juice during fermentation, the sweet smells that filled the room and overpowered those foolish enough to stand too long above the open top of a fermentation vessel. It was the rushing sound of the new wine as it was pumped through the tangled web of hoses from tank to tank to the oak barrel that would impart its final character. And it was the sound of a cork being pulled from the bottle, the comforting pop that sounded as the air rushed in, and the gurgling sound of wine being poured into the glass.

Clinking glasses around the table to salute one another's health was only part of the picture. The act also salutes the wine itself, our bridge from the human to the divine, our communion with a nature so expansive in its embrace that it could give us this life-sustaining beverage.

Ilsa stood her distance from me, gazing across the room as it filled with onlookers interested in watching Vito's crew at work. She smiled when she saw me looking back, but otherwise left me alone to resume my role as capo.

Behind me, half a dozen men were setting up tables in the half-light of the evening sun, and soon the tables were filled with baskets of bread and platters of food that had been prepared in kitchens nearby. There was the sound of corks popping, glasses being filled and then drained with satisfied sighs, and plates clattering as they passed from hand to hand. Vito's assistants descended the ladders leading up to the catwalk, and Vito came last.

We crowded around the rows of tables that were filled to overflowing with food and countless bottles of wine from previous harvests. The volume of the chatter rose, and stories were shared, sometimes in intimate ones and twos, sometimes loud enough to be certain that everyone could hear them. Most of the stories were told about these recent days of hard work; all of them were in good fun. Because during those days of relentless labor, heat, and stinging insects, we had all shared the benefits of family. We learned more about each other in the field, looked after each other in the rows between the vines, and fully intended to celebrate together as a family now that the work was done.

The party carried on into the night, cheers and salutes coming less often as the bottles were emptied, then everyone trooped off into the darkness that had settled around the winery on their way home. The work was done, and all could get a good night's rest — all except for Vito. As Ilsa and I walked arm-in-arm out the door of the winery, I caught the flicker of a light being switched on in the lofty air above the fermenters. In the dim light that strobed in and out in the rotating ceiling fan, I could just make out the image of a small, stocky man pressed up against the side of the open-top fermenter, peering inside to check on his new creation.

The Sweet Smell of New Wine

The next day I resumed my tour of the vineyards and estate property beyond the vines. I had much on my mind. I knew how Nonno Filippo had died, and why, if you could say that the sudden discovery of a half-brother and half-sister would be "why" he died.

It seemed so ironic, the way Vito and my grandfather had played together as children so many years ago. Then, as they grew up, each assumed different roles, but still in the same enterprise, an enterprise that was a blend of family and business. Maybe that's the way it is, inevitably, with Italian families, I thought. Business is so often shared with family, and family ties can make or break a business.

Thinking of Santo and Rita, I couldn't decide what I'd tell them. The rest of the family members and the employees of the Castello dei Trantini would soon lose interest in the murder theory, but I knew my cousins were still too engaged in the prospect of intrigue to let go of it easily. They would understand, I believed, if I told them the truth; but then would they? I wasn't sure whether they'd be more afflicted by the knowledge that they had as-yet undiscovered relations, or that the ever-trusted Vito was the villain.

Pondering these imponderables as I drove around the estate, I found myself drawn to the winery. There, in the clatter and noise of machinery being moved into position for the next phase, I could make out the husky voice of Vito barking orders to the staff just as he'd done for many years. He would be somewhere in the bowels of this vast building, putting his shoulder to a wheeled cart and pushing with all the strength of the younger men beside him, and directing their efforts with more breath than they had left after the exertion.

Vito could be strong as an ox when moving hoses, motors, and pumps, then as gentle as a finishing-school graduate when examining blends of the Trantini wines or teasing out a small sample of juice to run through its paces in the lab. Vito was the heart and soul of this winery; I knew it, and he did too.

Elena was nowhere to be found, but this wasn't surprising. She didn't work at the estate, although my recent discoveries left me thinking she could appear around a corner at any moment.

Stepping back out into the sunlight, Ilsa appeared from behind the trees to the left. She was wearing a brilliant-yellow, floral dress, with a scoop neck and loosely folded pleats down to a hem that cut across her knees. Her strawberry blond hair was gathered in a ponytail, and her simple makeup once again highlighted the natural beauty that had taken my breath away so many times.

Ilsa and I walked through the di Rosa vineyard, admired the slowly fading color of the leaves, and talked about how autumn was our favorite time of the year.

"The wine is in, and the work is easier," Ilsa said with a smile. I knew that line well; Nonno Filippo used it often to refer to this, his favorite time of the year also.

We wandered around the estate for some time, Ilsa with her arm linked with mine, and she strutted in a way that showed off her figure. I never forgot how much I loved to see her walk; I just had not had much opportunity to witness it in the recent days.

It seemed like we would never run out of things to say, stopping for a while under the spreading branches of an oak tree, then walking on again until we got to the Castello. We walked together through the private entrance reserved for family, and Ilsa whispered to me that she always knew this gate was here.

As we walked across the short distance from the gate to the main building of the Castello, Ilsa told me that she had been in love with me since she was fifteen. When I looked at her, she cast her eyes away, not as a coquette, but showing that she was a little embarrassed to reveal this intimacy, even to me.

Anita opened the door when she heard us coming, no longer displaying any surprise that Ilsa and I would be together, and we walked up to the wine library. It was five minutes after four o'clock, and Beppo had already set out the eight bottles to be tasted today. The corks were already pulled from the bottles, each resting in the mouth of the bottle from which it had come, and a glass was positioned right in front of each. I paused for a minute before beginning — truthfully, I had forgotten the time and didn't realize the table was already set.

As inconspicuously as she could manage, Anita went to the sideboard and gathered up eight more glasses and paired them up with the eight already lined up next to the bottles to be sampled. I looked at Ilsa, and she at me, and smiled.

When Anita had left the room, I began pouring the wine, a sample for each of us in the two glasses that stood in front of each bottle.

"*Ma, signore,*" Ilsa protested. "This is for you, the capo, to do."

"Capo" seemed distant for me, for a moment. Then I realized that Vito's denial of his inheritance turned the attention back to me.

Without answering her directly, I merely lifted the first pair of glasses, handed her one, and guided her toward the window overlooking the di Rosa vineyard. In that way, we worked through all eight bottles. It was, as Ilsa had indicated with her protest, probably the first time a woman had ever participated in this ritual at the Castello dei Trantini.

When sufficient time had elapsed to allow us to taste all the wines, Anita appeared once again bearing small bites of food, delicious morsels from garden and grill, savory samples combining the best flavors of Italy and filling the room with their fragrance. It was this last bit, the thought of non-wine aromas in this room, that made me pause. Anita must have seen the doubt on my face.

"Signor Filippo, it is not polite to serve wine to la signorina without sustenance," Anita said simply, and she left no doubt that she wasn't going to debate it, not even with the capo.

Ilsa and I relaxed for a while, still enjoying the scenery outside the window, and I went over the facts of Nonno Filippo's death once more.

"So, Elena is actually your grandfather's sister, and Vito is his brother?" she said, showing no less incredulity than she did the first time I told her the previous night.

"I guess so," I sighed but still couldn't decide what to do with the information.

"Should Vito get the Castello?" she continued. "He's the last surviving grandson."

I repeated what I had described the night before, understanding that Ilsa's question was a formality, as well as a longing for closure.

"Vito can't see a way to his inheritance. To declare that he is the 'last surviving grandson,' he must admit that his mother bore him and his sister out of wedlock. It's a well-known 'secret' but one that is buried in the past, which Vito would prefer not to resurrect at this point.

"And revealing the family connection also risks putting his sister in jeopardy, since the path to his inheritance was paved with her confrontation with Nonno Filippo."

I took Vito at his word, that he would rather continue to be the Trantino family winemaker than stir up suspicions that could cost both him and his sister their everlasting reputations.

Ilsa followed my words intently, smiling at times, thoughtfully reflecting at others. When I was done, we sat for a while longer and set the glasses down on the table. I chose the wine I liked best, then poured the remaining glasses into the dump bucket so that Beppo wouldn't be able to read my mind. Ilsa scrunched up her nose and asked what I was doing.

"You can taste wine with me, love," I said to her, cupping her chin in my hand, "but there are some secrets only the Trantini know." I laughed then, one of the most carefree laughs I had enjoyed for weeks.

La Dolce Far Niente

I spent a fair amount of time the next day by myself. I woke up late, fixed a double espresso and took my coffee cup and a plate of fresh rolls and fruit out onto the loggia to relax in the mid-morning light and eat my breakfast. There was very little activity in the vineyard below, about the first time since my return to the estate that everything was so quiet. I lounged around, enjoying the calm moments away from the winery and its employees, and took my time showering and getting dressed.

It reminded me of the Italian saying, "*La dolce far niente.*" Italians take a different view of their life and their world than do Americans. Italians are not at all lazy, but they believe that time to reflect and time to relax are necessary parts of life. *La dolce far niente* captures this spirit, and the Italians believe that it is, truly, sweet to have enough time in the day to do nothing, to relish the moment whether it be a solitary few minutes at a café, a lingering midday meal at a local trattoria, or stolen moments with a lover. I was beginning to recapture that spirit in the time since my return to Tuscany and the Castello, and I couldn't suppress a smile when I recognized it.

When I finally decided it was time to get going, I drove north to Florence. I had not spent much time there this visit, and I missed it. Arriving just before noon I went directly to the Piazza della Signoria, arguably the true center of the city, notwithstanding a similar claim to fame made by those fanatical about the nearby Chiesa di Santa Maria dei Fiori, called the Duomo.

I wound my way through the dwindling crowds of tourists at season's end and took a chair at La Borsa café.

As I sat, I glanced over at the next table and watched as a young couple giggled and whispered stories to each other, smiling broadly at their apparent pleasure. I thought of Ilsa and how we would have to come here together sometime soon. That day, I sat alone nursing a glass of wine and resting gratefully in the notion I was back home, because the Tuscan hillsides and vineyards were where I certainly belonged.

But as I contemplated the color of wine in the glass, I worked hard to decide what I should do next. I was undoubtedly the heir to the Castello dei Trantini. The question was not whether to accept the inheritance, but how to take control of so vast an enterprise with so little experience. Then I thought of Nonno Filippo and how his instructions over the years were intended to prepare me for this moment. I even thought of Vito, and how his recent comments had been meant to put me at ease, not only concerning his interest in the estate but also his confidence in me taking over.

With my eyes closed, I listened to the quiet sounds of daily life in Florence, the chattering of pedestrians, the smooth talk of waiters taking orders for espresso and cappuccino, the rub-rub of rolling tires on a bicycle going by. I inhaled deeply and breathed in the aromas of a classic European city, where scents of baked goods and roasted meat mingled with the effervescent smell of fresh flowers. Even the occasional whiff of cigarette smoke seemed in place in this menagerie of smells.

I rose, paid the bill, and walked on. I made my way toward the Palazzo Vecchio, framed now in the sliver of daylight between the buildings that sandwiched the café. As I emerged from the shadows, the towering edifice of the Palazzo before me, I walked directly to the spot where Savanarola had been burned at the stake. He was a seer, a monk who warned Florence of their sins in the fifteenth century, but he paid for his popularity with his life. But such was life in medieval times.

Life and death were not supposed to be so fickle in the twenty-first century.

I turned left onto the Via Calzaiuoli, past the Hotel Calzaiuoli, slowly making my way toward the Duomo, the grand cathedral that dominated the skyline of this majestic city. I walked past street vendors hawking jewelry and leather, past cafés with their espresso bars, past newsstands with a hundred magazines in a hundred languages. I stepped out into the Piazza del Duomo, into the bright October sun, and went to find my car.

As I drove back to the estate, I traveled down the roads I knew so well, cutting and twisting between the vineyards on the way back to Castelnuovo Berardenga. As I neared the property that belonged to my family, I knew what I would have to do.

By now, pedestrians along the roadway nearing the Castello who saw the Maserati approach knew whom to expect behind the wheel, and they waved and smiled at me. I drove up the winding, tree-lined hill to approach the Castello dei Trantini, then over the rise and back down the other side on a dirt road leading to the villa.

As I turned off the motor and pulled myself out of the car's leather seat, I looked up at the loggia. I could hear the soft clatter of dishes being set and a gentle humming, a song from my past, coming from the archway above the low wall surrounding the second-floor loggia. Ilsa looked out, paused in her song, and waved to me.

"*Ciao, amore. Hai fame?*" Ilsa asked, "Are you hungry?"

I mused about the alternative meanings of that question, then couldn't decide which one to answer, but the gleam in my eye must have caught her attention. Ilsa wagged a finger at me, then turned back to resume setting the table for dinner.

Castello dei Trantini

Santo and Rita arrived bright and early at the villa. They knocked on the wooden window frame at the entrance and brushed by me as soon as I pulled the door open.

"So, you were in such a hurry, and we haven't spoken since you ran out on us at Carlino d'Oro," Santo blurted out. I was certain that he had held the outburst in about as long as he could, but that time had expired.

"We know you know something," continued Rita, "so why don't you tell us. Nonno Filippo was murdered, wasn't he?"

I thought about how to answer the question and watched with some concern as Ilsa appeared in a very short robe from the bedroom. Santo's eyebrows raised, not so much because he was surprised by her presence, more that he was pleased to see her in such a state. Rita took little notice of Ilsa and continued to glare at me waiting for a response.

"*Sì*, I've found out much about Nonno Filippo's accident." I chose the words carefully, hoping to change the mood of the encounter with my selection of words.

"Nonno Filippo fell out the window of the wine library," I continued, but this revelation drew nothing but sneers from my cousins. Suddenly, Vito and Elena burst into the room. From his countenance, I could tell that Vito knew Santo and Rita had come for a showdown, and he wanted to be there to see what transpired.

"We don't know what happened," I said, looking directly into Vito's eyes, then diverting my gaze to Santo. "It's apparent that the fall was accidental just as the police said."

"How can you conclude such a thing?" Santo said with palms up-raised and brow knit into a look of confusion. "The police are idiots. How can you explain the mud stains on the rug?"

I thought for a long moment, and the room was so quiet that I could hear Ilsa's soft breathing just behind my ear. I looked from one person to another, then stared at the floor for a moment. The answer was slow to come, but I realized in a moment what I must say.

"Nonno Filippo's body wasn't discovered until the next morning," I said, and Rita made the sign of the cross as I said this. "In the meantime, Beppo had already come to clear away the bottles and empty glasses, a task he always accomplished an hour or two after our grandfather completed his tasting. Beppo entered the room perhaps around six o'clock without announcing himself, and he didn't expect to find any-one in the wine library. Of course, he was right because, by that time, Nonno Filippo had already fallen out of the window."

"But what does that prove?" asked Santo.

"Beppo was allowed entry to that room without knocking. That was his job, to take care of Nonno Filippo and his daily tastings. But Beppo also worked in the vineyard. As you recall, there had been some rain in the weeks leading up to the harvest, and the grounds were muddy."

Everyone in the room stared intently at me as I continued my re-counting of the scene.

"The next morning, Beppo reported for work as usual in the vine-yard. As he passed by the Castello, he heard a scream. He looked up from the veranda and saw Anita standing over a body. Even from a distance, he recognized the clothing. Without waiting to become in-volved with the accident scene, Beppo raced up to the wine library to see if anything had been disturbed since he was there the previous afternoon. Running into the room — and, remember, he never thought to knock since he was the only one allowed in there without asking permission — he ran straight for the wine tasting table, then to the window. In his panic, and in the state of confusion that he undoubtedly felt, he never stopped to check his boots. He didn't notice that he was tracking mud into Nonno Filippo's hallowed tasting room."

Everyone was silent. Santo and Rita looked at me with some doubt. Vito was wide-eyed and willing to accept this story. I couldn't see Ilsa since she remained standing just behind me, but I could imagine a satisfied smile and look of acceptance on her face.

"That's how it happened, eh?" said Santo, tilting his head as if barely struggling to believe me.

"Yes, that's the way it happened," I answered with finality.

Slowly, the four visitors turned toward the door and departed, my cousins muttering back and forth. Vito and Elena went without a word. I stood there, wondering about the story I had just spun for them — well, for two of them. I didn't get these details from Beppo. I didn't know whether he had returned to the wine library the next morning and didn't know — if he did — whether he would ever have worn muddy boots into that room. And I hadn't asked him yet whether he saw the muddy footprints the afternoon before, but I decided to let that fact fade away in this "investigation."

But I was sure of one thing: Santo and Rita were fair-weather private eyes. They were interested in a mystery as long as the mystery remained interesting. Filling their imagination with mundane details about workers with muddy shoes — Imagine! — I knew they would quickly lose interest in the chase.

As for Elena, I knew that she would rather bury the events of that afternoon so deep that no one would ever recover them.

And Vito, I didn't even have to ask. He was no doubt relieved that I had filled the void with a plausible story that would keep the investigators — not to mention the inquiring cousins — away from the truth and the threat of his sister being punished for the accident.

Mirelli? I found him waiting for me the next afternoon at the gate to the Castello.

"So, Signor Trantino, you're going to give up. Did you decide that Nonno Filippo's death was an accident?"

I wasn't sure what to tell him. Vito didn't want the Castello and winery. Filippo was his friend, his brother, and Vito didn't want anything that came by way of Filippo's death. He didn't even want his heritage made public, afraid that the wrong things would be said about the accident.

"*Sì, signore,*" I said. "It must have been an accident." And then I nodded and turned to walk back up the hill to the Castello.

Last of all was Ilsa. There was nothing to say to her. She knew the truth, and she knew me in my heart. I left the Castello grounds, exited through the secret gate that, by then, I realized wasn't so secret, and walked down the dirt road toward the villa. Ilsa would be waiting there — I knew she'd be there, now and for a long time.

As I mounted the steps that led up to the loggia, Ilsa stood waiting for me with a smile on her lips and a welcome embrace. We wrapped up tightly in each other's arms for a moment and turned toward the ledge. I locked my arm around her waist as we stared out at the di Rosa vineyards.

"Now what?" I asked.

"Now?" she asked, teasing me. "I guess we'll just have to see," and with that she planted a moist kiss on my cheek and drew me closer to her in the cool air of a Tuscan evening.

Acknowledgments

Every writer's story, whether fiction or fact, is grounded in some life experience. I would like to thank the Baron Francesco Ricasoli of Castello di Brolio for his gracious hospitality in letting me vacation on the grounds of the Castello that his family has called home since 1141. Living, even for a short while, in the embrace of the history and tradition of the Ricasoli family estate made the scenes of **A Death in Tuscany** come alive.

Dear reader,

We hope you enjoyed reading *A Death in Tuscany*. Please take a moment to leave a review in Amazon, even if it's a short one. Your opinion is important to us.

Discover more books by Dick Rosano at

https://www.nextchapter.pub/authors/author-dick-rosano

Want to know when one of our books is free or discounted for Kindle? Join the newsletter at http://eepurl.com/bqqB3H

Best regards,

Dick Rosano and the Next Chapter Team

About the Author

Dick Rosano is a wine, food, and travel writer with long-running columns in *The Washington Post*, *Wine News*, *Wine Enthusiast* and other magazines. He has five recent books on wine. *Wine Heritage: The Story of Italian-American Vintners* chronicles centuries of Italian immigration to America which laid the groundwork for the American wine revolution of the 20th century. His new series of mysteries is set in varying regions of Italy, featuring picturesque landscapes, intriguing characters, and the wine, food, and culture of the region. They include *Tuscan Blood*, *Hunting Truffles*, and *The Secret of Altamura: Nazi Crimes, Italian Treasure*. More on www.DickRosanoBooks.com. His travels have taken him to the wine regions of Europe, South America, and the United States.

In addition to his writing career, Dick has spent many years managing a highly trained team in global nuclear counter-terrorism.

Have you read? More books by Dick Rosano

Hunting Truffles
Northern Italy is the cradle for a precious culinary gem, the white truffle of Piedmont, worth more than gold and sought after by chefs and foodies alike. But this year, the truffle hunters are in a panic as they discover that their usual harvest has been stolen literally from under their feet. Inexplicably, the bodies of murdered hunters turn up, but no truffles. A young man from Tuscany, in tow with his aunt and her restaurant crew, pursue the theft and the thieves through the hills of Piedmont and the wine and food of Italy.

Secret of Altamura
It is 1943, and the Nazis control large parts of Italy. Colonel Anselm Bernhardt devotes his attention to stealing Italian art – and having his way with Italian women – but there is one great treasure that he covets even more.

In present day, his grandson swears to make amends for Bernhardt's crimes, but is bitten by the same temptation and averts his focus on reparation to search for the mysterious, historically vital treasure in southern Italy... a secret that can change the course of history.

Based on historical events, The Secret of Altamura takes you back to the cloud of terror that hung over wartime Italy, and invites you to explore the secrets and treasures that were hidden from the Nazi invaders.

You might also like:

Hunting Truffles by Dick Rosano

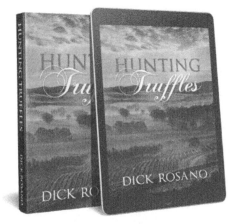

To read first chapter for free, head to:
https://www.nextchapter.pub/books/hunting-truffles

Made in the USA
Monee, IL
08 August 2022

11133893R20121